HEBE UHART

A QUESTION OF BELONGING

TRANSLATED FROM THE SPANISH BY
Anna Vilner

INTRODUCED BY
Mariana Enríquez

archipelago books

Published originally in Argentina by Adriana Hidalgo in 2020

English language translation © Anna Vilner, 2024

First Archipelago Books Edition, 2024

"The Preparatory School" appeared in *The New Yorker*, and "A Memory from My Personal Life,"
"Inheritance," and "Good Manners" appeared in *The Paris Review*.

Archipelago Books
232 3rd Street #A111
Brooklyn, NY 11215
www.archipelagobooks.org

Distributed by Penguin Random House
www.penguinrandomhouse.com
ISBN: 978-1-953-86180-1

Cover art: Photograph by Hans Hammarskiöld
© Hans Hammarskiöld Heritage

Frontispiece photograph: Nora Lezano

This work was made possible by the New York State Council on the Arts
with the support of the Office of the Governor and the New York State Legislature.

This publication was made possible with support from the National Endowment for the Arts,
the Nimick Forbesway Foundation, the Hawthornden Foundation, the Carl Lesnor Family Foundation,
the Jan Michalski Foundation and the New York City Department of Cultural Affairs.

This work has been published within the framework of the Sur Translation
Support Programme of the Ministry of Foreign Affairs, International
Trade and Worship of the Argentine Republic.

Obra editada en el marco del Programa Sur de Apoyo
a las Traducciones del Ministerio de Relaciones Exteriores,
Comercio Internacional y Culto de la República Argentina.

PRINTED IN CANADA

CONTENTS

INTRODUCTION

HEBE UHART LOVED to travel. Born in the town of Moreno, in the Buenos Aires province, she considered herself a writer of the outskirts. Her childhood home had been a sad one. An aunt who had severe psychiatric problems. A brother who died young. A little cousin, who she lost to a heart condition; another cousin, to a plane accident. Her mother suffered from depression. The hecatomb of grief. At a very young age, she became a rural school teacher. She'd bring the kids reading material; she would also bring them clothes. The school only offered primary education, and it was out in the country. One-story houses, this was back in the 70s. It was there, she told me in an interview, where she learned about the "things of life." "I was quite fickle and restless, I believed I could do things I couldn't. I had fits of wanting to do extraordinary things. Going to the country school helped me mature. I realized that I'd had my head in the clouds, dreaming of scholarships, of travels to Paris.

And I realized there were others who made sacrifices, who supported their homes. Who hitchhiked because they couldn't afford to take the bus. I was ashamed of my own thinking, of being so self-centered. It was then when I started to ripen. Some people never ripen, not even at 40. They go on demanding things and blaming their parents."

This was also when the urge to travel came over her, and she began doing so with her students. When she could, she traveled alone: to Bolivia by train, as a teenager, a journey not many girls would have taken at the time, but Hebe was so unlike most people I have met in my life: she was brave, curious, carefree, sure of herself. Yet, as a traveler, she didn't like going to big cities – they unsettled her (despite having visited many, of course). She preferred small towns. Places that were easy to get to know. Because what she loved was talking to people. These trips, day trips, in general (she referred to herself as a "domestic" chronicler) were a search for different ways of expression, a search that would take on the contours of the place itself.

Hebe Uhart's work as a collector of expressions and turns of phrase is a fortunate one for us, and important, because she is not merely a collector of the curiosities she observes, but a writer. Sometimes she learns things. In "Off to Mexico" she goes around Guadalajara, trying to understand the "thousands of things I'd read about and didn't understand, for example 'ni madres,' which is another way of saying, 'no way.' 'Ese viejo se las truena' (he's high) or 'vete a la

chingada,' (you'll be sent off to some distant, indeterminate place)."
In the crónica "Río is a State of Mind," she notes: "Cariocas do not
seem to care for categorical definitions, and they are not eager to
point out the difference between how things are and how they should
be. My conversations went more or less like this: 'There should be a
crosswalk on this street, it's a dangerous intersection.' Someone in
Portuguese: 'There should be one, yes, but there isn't.'"

Her fascination with language is not limited to the spoken: she
roams around cities and towns taking note of shop names, ads, and
graffiti, a routine that is repeated in almost every crónica. In "The
Land of Formosa," a newspaper helps her understand the place's
humor: "I only manage to read the literary supplement written by
readers of the paper. One person has written an ode to his eyeglasses,
praising their usefulness. The final line: 'Little lens, I love you so!' A
celebratory and grateful spirit abounds."

She is also concerned with the types of orality closest to literature
and another vital source is television. If Hebe Uhart had to be char-
acterized in one way, it would be by her complete lack of pretension
and artificiality, by her extreme discomfort when asked to carry out
the rituals of the consecrated writer. It would have never occurred to
her to discount television: such attitudes astonished her. One rainy
day in the capital city of Paraguay, Asunción, a city she adored, she
writes from inside her hotel: "The reporter on the bilingual channel

appears, speaking Guarani again. He blends it with Spanish and says 'satélite intersat.' He's clever like you wouldn't believe and moves around like an eel, or as if he had ants in his ass."

As traveler and chronicler, Hebe Uhart has her routines. She considers the hotel a refuge. If she goes to a neighboring city, for example, going back to the hotel is, for her, like going home. Another indispensable place is the café; if she doesn't spot one right away, she sets out on a desperate search. The café acts as a road stop: a place to light up a cigarette, flip through a newspaper, observe the regulars and those who pass by her window or table, if she happens to be sitting outside. She's stealthy, as well, and stays only for a short while: there is so much to absorb, no time to lose. Nevertheless, there is no sense of urgency in her crónicas. Her relationship to the places she visits and their people is easygoing: she knows that her presence is a curiosity, but she takes care not to intrude.

Whenever possible, she visits a residence, a school, a library; she talks to artists and local historians and looks for books that help her understand the place. A list of her cited authors and references would be endless; it would also be extremely eclectic: Charles Darwin and Domingo Faustino Sarmiento are usual referents; Alejandra Costamagna, Diego Zúñiga, and Alejandro Zambra, young Chilean writers, and friends of hers, show up in Santiago; she gives cameos to Peruvians Alfredo Bryce Echenique and Julio Ramón Ribeyro for being her favorites. In Asunción, she relies on Rafael Barrett and the great poet Elvio Romero; in Bariloche, local writers Luisa Peluffo and Graciela Cros; in Minas, Uruguay, her beloved Juan José Morosoli; in Guadalajara, the *Popol Vuh*. She barely mentions, however, her greatest influence: Fray Mocho, writer and journalist of the second half of the 19th century and the beginning of the 20th, who recorded popular porteño speech and the changing customs brought on by the population boom, and observed – with a sharp eye, playfully and without pretension – the society that fascinated him.

In interviews and library visits, Hebe Uhart consults local historians, those great forgotten or undervalued ones with whom she identifies. She buys their books and familiarizes herself with pioneer chroniclers and specialists, from Clifton Kroeber, author of *River Trade and Navigation in the Plata Region* to Miguel Donoso Pareja, who wrote *Ecuador: Identity and Schizophrenia*. She consults hundreds of books like these, both contemporary and academic, written by chroniclers from the 18th and 19th centuries. Uhart is voracious but offers all of this information considerately; she does not wish to overwhelm her readers, but to draw their attention to that which – due to its closeness – may have gone unnoticed by them. Each one of these crónicas is a sort of melancholic wake-up call, a gentle wave from the pampa, a hand that beckons and shows us that our own stories are complex, beautiful – we only need someone willing to listen.

I remember an anecdote, its setting a small town in the Buenos Aires province. This was where we became friends. I was, of course, a lot younger than she was. I don't feel as though I was the "chosen one." A lot of her friends were younger. She liked spending time with writers outside her generation. And it was easy to get to know Hebe because she enjoyed talking about flowers or politics more than literary prizes. Back to the anecdote: A tour guide from a town in the Buenos Aires province, one of those enthusiastic types she was drawn to, was leading her through the rooms of a country house. The guide was describing the climate and fauna of the region, showing her a pamphlet on local history. Hebe, her notebook near her face, was taking down notes with a pencil; her attention was fixed although her gaze seemed scattered, she was so curious and wanted to see everything. Once the tour was over, she thanked the guide warmly. When she left the house, her only comment was: "Did you hear how she referred to the indigenous people? She said they were completely tame Indians."

She found the guide's statement wrong, racist, of course. But she also found it interesting. And she didn't judge. She knew that the most important thing, always, was to try to understand.

In the final years of her life, the oeuvre of Hebe Uhart received a very particular kind of recognition. Her story collections and novellas moved from independent presses to corporate publishing houses such as Alfaguara. When it came to her nonfiction, she chose to stay loyal to smaller publishers and, if she had an unedited piece, she preferred to send it to a press run by young people. There was a waiting list to get into her writing workshop and her stories were adapted into theater performances. She seemed to be unfazed by it all and went on having barbecues on her terrace. Ricardo Enrique Fogwill, one of the finest and most renowned (and unruly) Argentine writers, once said: "Hebe is the best writer in Argentina," and everyone agreed wholeheartedly (and whoever didn't yielded to the charismatic Fogwill). I told her this in her apartment in Almagro, while she served us limoncello, a gift from a student in her narrative workshop. She opened the window to her balcony, which was filled with gorgeous plants, azaleas, bougainvilleas, and said:

"Bah."

Followed by:

"If you write, and your writing's good, soon enough you'll be recognized. Look, how could I be the best writer in Argentina – what does that mean? Nothing."

Writer and teacher Pía Bouzas, a former student of Hebe's and one of her closest friends, has a theory about the renaissance of her work, which came after years of being overlooked:

"Beyond her effort and perseverance, I believe that readers came to her. Younger writers began to observe the world as she did, to consider the details, the off-kilter, to go off the beaten track of the born-and-bred writer. She found a path outside this masculine Argentine tradition, which isn't only referring to male writers, but also to a way of using language. This is aligned with her search for younger writers. She deals with important themes – immigration, family, the Argentine – but she does so with a lighter touch."

Hebe Uhart shared her autobiography in small doses. At times it was simply a remark, other times she offered something personal. But she never wrote, for example, about the death of her brother. She was reticent about her financial situation, too. It is necessary to point out that Hebe Uhart was not a writer endowed with resources, she did not plan these trips on a big budget. On certain occasions, she was invited to a book fair or a writers' conference or some university talk: she left a record of these invitations not only as a thank you to her hosts but also to emphasize that we are dealing with a precarious writer. Some are trips she had been sent on. Others she paid for herself, and she didn't hesitate to comment on the modesty of the hotels she stayed in. She was also over 70: she wandered, chatted, and saw as much as her body would permit, and she was not one to hide these limitations. We do not encounter an adventurous travel writer taking on the wildness of nature, of institutional violence or crime, but rather a writer and philosophy professor who needed to take inventory of her obsessions.

For the Argentine writer and journalist María Moreno, "the best question is the one that seems to appear from nowhere; it provokes something in us, and it is only through the provocation that we discovered that it was the right question asked at the right time." Hebe Uhart discovered that this sudden question, in her case, was almost always tied to animals. Partly because it helped break the ice, but also because the writer found what she was looking for in the answer: ways of expression she's never heard before. And the language of those surrounded by animals is utterly delightful. Don Roque from "Irazusta" in the Entre Ríos province, says: "Our animals are very clever. The cows moo like crazy when something serious happens; they moo if they lose a calf or miscarry, and the others surround the mother gently. . . Baby goats cry like children." And often her follow-up question would be about politics or some local attribute that seeks confirmation or denial.

I remember a strange encounter between Hebe and an animal. It was at the Frankfurt Book Fair, in 2015, I believe. Hebe had prepared and neatly printed out all of her lectures. But she didn't stay at the fair the entire day; a wanderer, curious as she was, she wanted to see the city. The Argentine delegation was staying at a hotel across from the train station, and we ended up spending a lot of time there: she liked the market inside, with its Turkish stalls, the very friendly man selling beer and trying to make himself understood, the Chinese food counter. A station is a contained world and Hebe Uhart liked contained worlds, with their own rituals and languages, although everyone spoke German and not being able to understand them exasperated her a little. One evening before returning to the hotel, after a very abundant dinner, we paused in front of a boy of around twenty who appeared to be living in the street and sleeping at the station with his pet ferret, that animal with a pointed snout and affectionate eyes, domesticated but slightly wild. Hebe stopped in front of the animal, and pointed:

"Cuis!" she said, loudly.

The boy stared at her, bewildered.

The cuis is an animal from the Argentine pampas, similar to a ferret, maybe more like a mouse.

"Cuis!" she repeated, clearly this time, as if this would facilitate their communication. "Is it a cuis, yes or no?" She was let down when she found out that no, it wasn't. She stayed for a while, playing with the little animal and attempting to chat to its owner. Hours later, very early in the morning, she found a taxi to take her to the zoo. She couldn't convince any of the other writers to go with her, not even me, who, victim of my own obsessions, went to see the cemetery. But Hebe Uhart wasn't offended by things like that. Her visit to the monkey house, she told us when she returned to the hotel at noon, had been fabulous.

In the last years of her life, Hebe Uhart read as much fiction as nonfiction, but she preferred writing crónicas, she used to say, because she felt that what the world had to offer was more interesting than her own experience or imagination. This gesture is a political one: to go outside oneself, to encounter others. The gesture was accompanied by a subtle frustration when she felt that others, in some way, were being robbed of their dignity. The political stance of these crónicas is apparent: their Latin American anchor, the recovery of ignored or undervalued stories – local histories, everyday wisdom, ways of expression – and at the center, often, is one of her favorite subjects: the indigenous peoples of the continent.

In "The Land of Formosa," for example, she visits a school in the Toba community, and later a university. She wants to see how bilingual and bicultural education is carried out, but more than that, Hebe Uhart believes in institutions. She was a teacher all of her life and this progressive imprint is evident. "I spoke with two literature students; one of them, Victor, was ethnically Toba. Victor wrote poetry in both Spanish and Toba, with epigraphs by Aristotle and Sartre. He hesitated for a while before sharing his writing with me, observing me with his large dark eyes while he rustled around in his backpack, as if he were buying himself more time."

Hebe examined mestiza America and confronted the racism that attempted to negate this reality, challenged it by saying: to speak of the native peoples, white people must first admit how little they know. She did not do this from a position of moral superiority or miserabilism. She simply went to communities and asked questions. She found out how people live in the now, she reconstructed their histories and tried to shed herself of prejudices. She writes: "In my travels I strengthened my belief that this world is made of mixture and, in all the communities I visited, I found the old mixed in with the new: technology is everywhere. . . the great cacique Cafulcurá had more captives than natives in his encampments and, of all those relationships and mutual learning, there has been very little left of a written record. So I wanted to find out more about the people who, keeping in mind most of Latin America, form more than half of our population."

There are not too many examples of writers in contemporary Argentine literature who show interest in indigenous people. Hebe herself, who largely avoided self-reference, confides in "A Trip to La Paz," a piece that evokes her first trip abroad when she was twenty years old. In a train bound for La Paz, accompanied by a friend who resembles the actress Jeanne Moreau, she roams the hallways, seduces some young Peruvians, bumps into a priest who used to be her neighbor. Then she comes across an Andean teacher. The woman's clothes seem inappropriate to her and she feels "like the superior tourist." The teacher, who is traveling with her little son, tells her about the tree trunks students sit on, that there is no chalkboard. "When she spoke, she was overcome by a kind of indignation that made me see her dignity." When they cross the border, the teacher takes out a Bolivian flag and gives it to the child. The two of them say "viva Bolivia!" Then, Hebe writes: "I wasn't the least bit politicized back then; I didn't even read the newspaper. . . Years later, I began to read literature about dependence and liberation, about spears and flames; in short, about everything that was happening in the world. I read with the passion of the enlightened, like I had finally found my place. Of course I am left with only a general idea of everything I read, but I've never been able to forget the Bolivian teacher, not for all these years." This is how, without pretension, she narrates her epiphany, her political awakening.

Hebe Uhart evaded the autobiography. Very few of her crónicas feature her as protagonist; there are, however, two that stand out. The first has the revealing title "A Memory from My Personal Life," a brief look at a romantic relationship with Ignacio, an alcoholic boyfriend from her youth; although she always spoke of him, she almost never wrote about this intense man. But the most important unedited piece is without question "My Bed Away from Home," published originally in the supplement Radar Libros from Pagina/12 on October 21st, 2018, days after her death. A story of her days at the hospital, when she was already very sick, it is prodigious in its observation and truly unusual in its absence of sentimentality.

Hebe would have been a little annoyed at the adjective "moving," but her writing inside the ICU, as she discusses inclusive language with Colombian residents, is moving, and proof of her defiant personality. "I spent all of my time in the ICU thinking of the bathroom and its whereabouts, as though it were London or Paris. After being transferred to Intermediate Care, they situated me near an EXIT sign which, to my great joy, was directly beside a bathroom. I felt as though I had been promoted, and what's more, I also began taking walks along an external corridor with the help of several meters of rope." Elvio Gandolfo, an Argentine writer and contemporary of hers, says that Hebe had her own style of looking, and that this style provoked her way of writing. And since her gaze was tender and playful, but also relentless, she was able to write passages like this one, full of humor and intelligence, two months before she died. Never, not even when she was writing her final words and could have granted herself permission to do so, did she give into the temptation of navel-gazing. She always put dignity first. The dignity of others, and her own.

MARIANA ENRÍQUEZ
translated by Anna Vilner

A QUESTION OF BELONGING

A MEMORY FROM MY PERSONAL LIFE

ABOUT THIRTY YEARS AGO, I had a boyfriend who was a drunk. Back then, I was full of vague impulses and concocted impossible projects. I wanted to build a house with my own two hands; before that, there'd been another project, involving a chicken hatchery. I was never cut out for industry or manual labor. I didn't think that alcoholism was a sickness – I believed he would be able to stop drinking once he decided to. I was working at a high school and had asked for some much-needed time off to improve my mental health, and I spent my days with my drunken boyfriend going from club to club, and from one house to the next. We paid countless visits to the most diverse assortment of people, among them an old poet and his wife who would receive guests not at their home, but in bars. Some turned their noses up at the pair, whispering that it took them a week to get from Rivadavia Avenue to Santa Fe Avenue, as they spent a full day at each bar. It was a year of great discovery for me, learning about these people and their homes, but sometimes it was boring because drunks have a different sense of time and money. It is like living on a ship, where time is suspended, and as for my boyfriend's friends, they were always destined for the bottle and stranded at the bar (or so they claimed) until someone could come rescue them. I used to get bored when drunk poets began counting the syllables of verses to see if they were hendecasyllabic, trochaic… it could go on for hours.

The whole time I was mixed up in all of this, nobody ever knew where I was going. I would only come home to eat and sleep – I didn't tell my family anything. They became concerned. My mom had a cousin follow me and report back to her:

"They sleep at a different house every night. My advice – buy her an apartment."

My mom gave me all her savings (one million pesos, the equivalent of twenty-five thousand dollars) and told me to find an apartment. So my boyfriend and I went together to choose. I would confront people and ask them questions while he hung back, watching me work. Before long we came to an old but giant apartment with a long hallway. "Look at all this space!" I said, thrilled. But there was something strange about it – the wall dividing the apartment from the one next to it was very low (about ten observers looked at us from the other side). I thought: "No big deal, we can raise the wall later. With all this space, we could get new wallpaper, remodel…

Right?" He said yes to everything because being around so many people terrified him – neither of us knew how to remodel anything. As usual, he looked on fearfully, with admiration, as I confronted people. I felt strong and confident, like an executive. So I hadn't built the chicken hatchery after all, but I had discovered an interesting hobby. Luckily, I was advised not to buy the apartment. I bought a very old two-bedroom, with a telephone and an elevator that had never been used. A piece of the ceiling had crumbled, so we put the bed in a small foyer beside the front door, a decision we'd agreed upon. The owners had sold me the apartment without cleaning it: when I swept, a cloud of dust would form. So, I told myself: "No need for sweeping. After so many years, it can't help but stay dirty." I had already gone back to work and was performing well, but I was tired of coming home to two or three drunks who had kept me awake the night before arguing about the poetry of Góngora or Quevedo, sleeping on the floor of one of our vacant rooms. I could never bring myself to say "Get out of my house."

Instead, I began to focus my energies on curing my boyfriend: I would take him to the doctor, the psychologist, and buy his vitamins for him. After much preparation, he was finally ready for his first job interview; he had agreed to everything, but it didn't progress any further than that. He never did sober up, but I at least learned how to buy and sell apartments.

A TRIP TO LA PAZ

WHEN I WAS TWENTY years old, I went abroad for the first time; the train to La Paz took three days and it was easy to meet people on board. I went with Julia Leguizamón, who was a few years older than I was. To me, she was the essence of mystery and refined intelligence – qualities I lacked. She had an air of Jeanne Moreau about her and was always lounging on her bunk bed. When she did come down it was as if she had no choice but to do so, as if the world was oppressing her with its tedious demands. She said the most clever and fascinating things without glancing away from her little mirror, and plucked invisible hairs like a queen exiled from her country; left without a servant to take care of such inferior chores, she was eternally humiliated to be fending for herself. I admired how naturally she expressed her ideas (revelations that I would've announced to the whole train) and how she reflected on her mysterious past.

Once we passed a café I wanted to go into.

"Not this one," she said. "It's haunted."

I took the statement literally. *Does she actually believe in ghosts?* I thought, and said something, timidly, to that effect. She clarified that she meant it symbolically and I didn't ask anything more. It wasn't the right time.

She didn't roam the train with me, while I took several routes, several times a day, looking at my reflection in the windows as I walked. I wore a red and white striped T-shirt with jeans; it was my uniform, and roaming the train was a kind of mission – the train called to me. The first day of the trip, I met two Peruvian guys who studied medicine in Buenos Aires and were heading home for the holidays. I must have told them which cabin we were in, since Julia never left; that way the older brother could chat with her and the younger one, who was my age, could stay with me. He reminded me of a dark-skinned version of my brother, and it occurred to me how extraordinary it would be if my brother could change colors instead of always being the same monotonous skin tone. He told me he was the descendant of an Inca prince (I later verified that every self-respecting Peruvian who looks the part descends from an Inca prince), but I didn't know whether to believe him or not. After so much talk of the Inca Empire, of Argentina and Peru, he invited me to sit on his lap (we were in a narrow corridor of the train and he was sitting on a sort of stool in the corner). My response to this flirtation was to walk away quickly, to bound through the cabins as if nothing had happened.

Julia, in her own way, had started chatting with the older brother. He was on the bottom bunk and she was lounging above him, high and unreachable like a queen. I didn't catch much of what they said, because I was used to kids being excluded from adult conversations, but she believed her words and wisdom should be denied no one. Despite her lying on the bed, it was clear that the whole situation was respectful, and that the Peruvian considered her to be a fountain of wisdom too. By the second day, the brothers' presence was more sporadic. One must have said to the other: "All talk and no action."

While roaming the other end of the train, I found Father Werner in second class, surrounded by countless baskets and boxes. I was ten the last time I saw him, but he looked at me as though it had been only yesterday. Back then, when he was the assigned priest of Moreno, town gossips said he had been exiled from his former church. He was known for his peculiar habits: to reach the altar more quickly, and to avoid traversing the room where the sacristan slept, he made a breach in the other wall and would enter bowing, his ornaments in hand. He lived off bananas and chocolate, which he would eat while riding his bicycle everywhere, so he wouldn't waste any time.

When my brother was twelve or thirteen, he stole money from the house and gave it to Father Werner – it was for some experiments he was conducting by the riverbanks to find a cure for cancer. While he was down there, he would occasionally study the flora and fauna as well. He visited us at home one day and told my mom the story of how he escaped Nazi Germany. He said he had joined a cycling race, disguised as one of them. If he really did escape as a cyclist, I wondered, where did he put his clothes and suitcase? Every traveler has a suitcase, but it seemed that those who fled the war were different from the rest of us. My family thought of him as the hero of a Greek tragedy, and we were like the chorus watching him with reproach, admiration, and awe. He dipped a vanilla cookie into a glass of liqueur while he told his incredible story and drank the whole concoction down just like that. He probably thought that everything mixed up in the stomach and that as long as it wasn't poison, it was edible. But these were people who lived through the war, so of course they were different. My brother was forgiven for taking the money; in the end, it had been for a noble cause.

Some said Father Werner was banished from Moreno because he let his parishioners wear shorts to mass. So they sent him to another town, where no one looked at their neighbor in church. They would listen to the service intently, even if there happened to be an elephant beside them. What a surprise it was to find Father Werner in second class among a group of Qulla, sitting on a slatted wooden bench and surrounded by baskets. Not even a blink when he saw me after ten years, as if he had been expecting me. He asked if I was traveling in the sleeper and I said yes, which made me feel a bit awkward since he, a priest, was traveling in second class with so many boxes in tow. He asked if he could store his boxes in our room. I told him I had to ask my travel companion.

Soon after, the train stopped for a long while and Julia got out because her legs were cramping (she only moved when there was an urgent need to do so). In no time at all, Father Werner appeared beside us, surrounded by his boxes. I thought about what he might be carrying, if he was moving – seeing as he was always on the move – or if he might have chickens or gold with him. Personally, I didn't want him to put those boxes and baskets in our room. What if the nomadic priest had dirty robes? (Cleanliness did not seem to be his specialty.) And what if the whole room began to reek? It's not that I noticed any grime on him, nothing was visible – it wasn't possible to discern if he was clean or dirty. Julia, gesturing like an empress who couldn't be bothered by something as trivial as boxes, gave him permission to put them in our room. On the one hand, I admired someone so elegantly generous, and, on the other, I didn't tell her what I knew about the Father, because something inexplicable told me that doing so might have gotten in the way of his mission. Those boxes would be an obstacle to my train excursions – not a problem for her, considering she came down from her bunk about once a year.

But now the train was stopped and we were talking to him on the platform. He took out a sort of pendulum – he said that it measured positive energy – and swung it equally in front of our chests. I didn't trust the device and I looked at it how Indians first looked at the compass, which they called the "dizzy needle." When I had finally given up on trying to understand that man (it's impossible to understand someone who is capable of anything), he began talking about hunting chinchillas. He made it seem like it was a hypothetical adventure and I didn't know if he was going to hunt them, if we would hunt them for him, or if we would all go hunting together.

It was like this: first you had to get in with an Indian who knew the land and how to avoid threats and hindrances like weather, vermin, and the law. I don't know at what point or from where, but he took out a beautiful book about chinchilla breeding that captivated Julia, as if she had spent her whole life hunting critters. The book hadn't come from one of the baskets and this was another peculiarity of his: all of a sudden, some topic or object would appear and then disappear. Did Father Werner offer books on chinchillas in the same way he offered holy cards or bananas and chocolate? It was clear he won over disciples, first my brother and now Julia. Once we crossed the border he disappeared without a trace. I don't know exactly when he took the boxes from our room.

I continued roaming the train, one end to the other, in my jeans and red and white striped shirt. I needed a break, so I sat down in front of a young woman and her baby in second class. The woman was wearing a worn-out, smoky-blue suit and carried a purse of the same color. She was in heels. Her outfit seemed inappropriate for the journey and I felt like the superior tourist. We smiled at each other. Her smile was cautious, as if she'd be ashamed to widen it too much. Her purse, her suit, and the child she was holding were all immaculate (the child's dark skin was gleaming, just like his little shoes). Something in that incongruity between the sad, worn-out shade of blue and her cleanliness interested me, and we began to talk. She was a teacher like I was and taught classes in a public school on the outskirts of La Paz. She told me that the school couldn't afford chairs for the students and that they sat on tree trunks; chickens would circle nearby and distract the kids. They didn't have a map, a chalkboard, or anything. "Meanwhile private schools," she said, "have every luxury there is." I quit judging her inappropriate outfit. When she spoke, she was overcome by a kind of indignation that made me see her dignity. The conversation became more fluid after that. She took a chicken breast from her bag and cut it up into small pieces for the child.

"Eat, honey," she said.

Again I thought it was inappropriate to bring chicken on such a long trip (we were at the border and she was going to La Paz); but she sliced it so carefully that I changed my mind – it was fine to eat chicken on the train after all. I began to think about our similarities and differences. Both of us were teachers (I was just starting out), but while she lived off her poor salary, I spent mine on travel and buying whatever bullshit caught my eye. I didn't plan on being a teacher for the rest of my life, and, what's more, I taught at a school that had everything paid for by the government. I didn't want to improve anything at my school; I'd rather have burned it to the ground because the principal had it in for me. The way she hounded me was unbearable: she'd scolded me twice already for putting my briefcase on the desk. This woman, on the other hand, requested that the authorities send her maps, books, benches, and milk for her students. We had barely crossed the border when she took out a little Bolivian flag and gave it to the child.

"Say, *Viva Bolivia*, son."

She, the child, and I said, "Viva Bolivia" and her smile widened sadly. It was like a gift for me.

I wasn't the least bit politicized back then; I didn't even read the newspaper. I went back to my room and forgot about her with the characteristic indifference of young people to experience and forget in the same instant. The encounter with her was interesting, like the ones with Father Werner or the Peruvian brothers. But there were so many more to come! Years later, I began to read literature about dependence and liberation, about spears and flames; in short, everything that was happening in the world. I read with the passion of the enlightened, like I had finally found my place. Of course I am left with only a general idea of everything I read, but I've never been able to forget the Bolivian teacher, not for all these years.

THE PREPARATORY SCHOOL

DRIVEN BY NECESSITY, I accepted a substitute teaching position for Latin in the National School of Buenos Aires, an elite preparatory school. I never thought that I would teach high school Latin, although I was equipped to do so. And concerning the substitution: they didn't explain if the teacher I was filling in for was sick or had died or been fired; his absence sounded more like a time-out. It was not only time that seemed frozen; the school did, too. Something had sucked the air out of that place: at school functions, students did not breathe, and the teachers' lounge featured enormous portraits of illustrious rectors, plus a gigantic one of a major naval battle. The teachers' lounge was dark, the courtyards too, and in those places I would sense disapproving looks aimed in my direction.

Surely there must have been a modern methodology for teaching

Latin, but that place prevented me from making any plans. I would go in terrified and only feel calm again once I got two blocks away. I felt that everything I did was wrong; my fear was a kind of animal fear, and I was just relieved that they didn't beat me or lock me inside.

The school has always been a nest for fledgling leaders, dissidents, and success stories, but, at thirteen and fourteen years old, those kids were punished for any little thing; a security guard, who was said to be with the police, did not allow them to go to the bathroom during classroom hours, no exceptions. These were the conditions I had to work in, and teaching Latin no less. The sentences the students translated went like this:

> The slave prepares a dinner of roasted eel for the lady.
> The dog must be obedient to his owner, the child to his parents.
> Young lady, put on the light-blue toga to honor our goddess.
> Caesar advances forty-five parasangs with his Army.

How far is a "parasang"? Who could I ask?

> Young lady, you must put flowers on the goddess's altar and cinnabar on Janus's.

What might "cinnabar" be? The students were going to fuck with me by asking, but neither I nor they actually wanted to know. Having made a fool of myself, I would leave the school still not knowing such things, and if, as I expected, some punishment were to be inflicted on me, at least I would know the reason. The texts used such restrictive and cruel language; it was always an order, a demand, an altar for some goddess. But the passage I hated most was the one by Arria, the matron who, with great conviction, told her sick husband in one room that their son, who had died in another, was getting better and had eaten a hearty meal.

Since I taught Latin class from 11 a.m. to 1 p.m., I would lighten the mood by teaching Roman culture in the second hour and describing what the Romans ate.

One thing I always found odd about Roman cuisine was that one creature was cooked inside another. For example, you might find a goose inside a pig, and, inside the goose, a little chicken, all of this smeared in honey, the glue that kept it together.

I would say to my students: "How interesting!"

And their reply: "Disgusting! Why are you telling us this – and right at noon!"

I also taught them that, in ancient Rome, people would dump everything in the streets, piss and all the rest. The lesson generated such an uproar that I wasn't able to contain it. I was saved by the bell, but the security guard who was with the police still came in and stared at me. I fled to a café about five blocks away and outside my regular route; I wandered around like a lost puppy. When I sat down, the café seemed extraordinary to me, the street like a sanctuary, and the waiter a prince.

GOOD MANNERS

YESTERDAY I WAS RIDING the 92. The bus was half-empty and a woman of about sixty or seventy caught my eye. It was difficult to get a sense of her age, or her social class. Could she be poor? No, but she didn't seem rich either, nor did I pick up on any of that visible effort the middle class puts into their appearance: dressing neatly, in complementary colors. Her clothes reminded me, more than anything, of someone trying to go incognito. She didn't come off as a housewife; I decided she had the look of a government inspector. She sat down beside me.

"Señora, I'm getting off at Pueyrredón," I said, so I wouldn't have to get up if her stop was before mine.

"Works for me," she said, "I'm getting off at Laprida."

She settled in beside the window as though she owned the seat and was allowing me to sit beside her. The bus driver was a young, pudgy guy, but agile. He drove expertly and very fast, which I noticed when he passed the other 92 (they tend to run two or three at a time, the drivers amusing themselves by racing). He changed gears smoothly, as though he'd been born at the steering wheel. "Whoa!" he said, suddenly. I asked what happened. My neighbor, looking straight ahead at nothing in particular, said, "She shouldn't have crossed from the right."

Her tone was cold and dry and I felt ignorant. I hadn't noticed anyone crossing.

"She pulled it off," the driver said. "What a brave girl – sometimes girls are brave."

I didn't know what to say because it isn't every day that a bus driver speaks. I also didn't understand why the girl had been brave for crossing.

"Yes," said my neighbor, the inspector, "But she could end up in a tree."

This sounded a lot like prophecy, or a desire that the girl end up in a tree. The driver cracked a smile, he found something funny in the statement. A woman got on the bus; she greeted the driver, he returned the greeting. I wanted to feel worthy of my seat, so I said something about their civility – I wanted the inspector woman to accept me. I referred to their greeting as an old-fashioned custom.

"It's good manners," she said, without looking at me.

It seemed that good manners, to her, did not have to do with doing polite things to make life more pleasant, but were things of divine origin. The driver spoke again: "There's a traffic jam. Someone double parked."

"That's not allowed," she said.

He spoke to her, even though he didn't care much about good manners. I would never have known where and how to park.

"There it is. Over there, at Bazterrica Hospital," he said.

She replied yet again. I felt a growing need to say something to the driver, partly to appear less ignorant and partly to take advantage of the rare opportunity to talk to a bus driver. So I said something that I immediately regretted: "Sir, do you like it when people greet you?"

I regretted asking because I figured the woman was going to condemn my question.

"When it's one or two, have at it, but when it's about a hundred who greet me, I start thinking they want something," he said.

"It's good manners," the woman insisted.

I wanted to ask the driver another question so I could join their conversation, but even as the questions formed in my mind, they already seemed trivial. Despite knowing I was headed toward being ostracized, I said "How often do you take this route every day?"

"Four times."

He answered me curtly, even though he wasn't the curt type. Evidently, he was speaking only with her. I had another question up my sleeve: where did the 92 come from and where was it going? I genuinely would have liked to know. But it seemed so irrelevant (and my seat mate's silence ever so deafening) that I kept quiet. Her silence made me feel like I was six or seven years old again, playing with a nutty girl I knew: every time I went to do something – swing in the hammock or take off running – the girl would stomp her foot angrily and say "No!" It made me feel like I was perpetually in the wrong. Everything that I did or stood for was – to that girl – bad. But things were different now. I no longer felt thrashed, like a wind-beaten plant, by that uncomfortable feeling. I had built up my defenses. When we got to Pueyrredón, I avoided every possible show of good manners: I got off the bus without saying goodbye to either of them.

ANIMALS

IT IS SAID THAT ANIMALS resemble their owners, and I see proof of this when I look around my neighborhood: an imposing, burly man, who would be quite attractive if not for his permanent grimace, walks his large dog on a leash. He is uncompromising, in control of himself, composed. The dog also seems composed, but composure on him looks a bit like resignation.

Another woman, with a whimsical face and a look of blissful ignorance, has a tiny puppy with bulging eyes and its tongue stuck out; it hops around like a little bird.

A slender and pretty girl walks a black-and-white greyhound that seems as proud of his appearance as his owner; she is probably on a diet and gives her dog low-fat food too, to keep his figure in check. One can find food for all types: skittish cats, aging and overweight dogs, frail pregnant cats, etc. But I am struck by a very short and skinny man and his tiny dog: he does not appear to have the resources to buy diet dog food, but he probably gives him the best he can within his means. The dog seems to have been thoughtfully chosen – small, so as not to take up much space (or knock over his owner). They go on long walks while the owner talks to him nonstop. Once, in passing, I heard him say: "First we'll go to the grocery store, then to the bakery."

I get the feeling the man is spiritual and in possession of knowledge that, for some reason or other, he is unable to act on. He is courteous and always waves hello, but also solitary. During the long conversations with his little dog – whom he would never call "my pet" – he tells stories from his life; about, for instance, the time he worked at El Noble Repulgue. And he tells his dog that once things get better, he will buy him a new little wrap (the dog's wrap is now the same color as his body and seems to be a part of him, like the owner's overcoat) to shield him from the world of towering men who crush you with their very presence, from the relentless horns and wailing sirens that tell us disaster is on its way.

INHERITANCE

WHEN I USED TO TAKE walks along Bulnes Street and Santa Fe Avenue, a certain boutique would catch my eye. It always displayed the same series of colors: beige, dusty rose, baby blue – a modest array of colors – and always the same ones on rotation, never a red or a yellow. Everything behind the display window was elegant, but hidden in shadows; this included the owner, who seemed determined to fulfill her duties despite having so few customers. The owner's silent manner and her desire to go unnoticed (as if showing one's face were distasteful) led me, in one way or another, to this idea: she must have inherited her taste in clothing from her mother and she was making sure to carry on its legacy. Well done, well done on that display window, but with so few customers, the shop was doomed.

On Corrientes, at the corner of Salguero, there is another window displaying sweaters paired with little vests (for when it gets chilly).

Every week, the owners debut a new line of muted colors: grayish blue, blush, timid yellow. Delicate T-shirts that seem to say: this is the way things are. The garments are always the same shape and length; every week, the owners change the color scheme. It occurs to me that this taste is also inherited, passed down from a time when women dressed to please rather than offend, and when dialogues unfolded like this:

"Go ahead, dear."

"You first, I insist."

"How kind of you."

"Let's catch up, darling!"

As a friend of mine says, such women used to talk as if they'd made a pact at birth.

Nobody goes into that shop either, they go into the shop next door that sells skirts with studded red flowers, asymmetrical ones, others with ruffles. Because nobody cares about offending others these days, nobody cares much about anyone. Which is why the vendors at the shop with the muted colors don't mind if their clothes sell or not; passersby call their sweaters "dainty little things." One is inspired to buy those outfits and dress up in a different color every week, like the display window, to harmonize the soul, to have things change without really changing, to perform a ritual that ensures eternity.

Some dogs can be inherited, as can photos, promises, and schedules. The way one decorates one's house is inherited, too. I once visited a house where everything was smooth and shiny as a bocce ball, not a painting or flower vase in sight. I hovered from room to room like a low-flying plane. This was because, in another house, the department of hygiene had come to get rid of some rats, bats, or kissing bugs. These problems no longer existed, but the fear survived.

In houses full of folders from bygone days, the ancestors are present: they talk to each other, folder to folder, handkerchief to the doll on the bed. Certain ideologies are inherited as well. Some families are progressives, Peronists, others are communists. As much as they might deny the ideologies of their ancestors, many will inherit their customs and tastes. Families that come from the progressive tradition tend to have good taste. They do not flaunt their wealth, tend to be discreet about the real estate they own, critique mindless spending because it's unbecoming, and if they are professionals, let's say doctors or dentists, they have paintings of horses galloping in the office, but it's always a discreet gallop, nothing out of control.

In Peronist families, whims and desires are more permissible. If a member of the family has a craving for hot chocolate at four in the morning, or spends all of their savings on meeting Mickey Mouse in Disneyland, or shoots down loquats with a gun, the other family members will not openly disapprove, because they are not inclined to make value judgments – they are not constrained by the Platonic Form of the Good.

The most curious houses belong to the descendants of communist resistance fighters. Even if these heirs no longer fight or say they don't give a damn about politics, their homes contain the traces of revolutionary spirit. They cannot bear to dress sharp or get dolled up because that would mean assuming a privilege that is at odds with the proletariat. Their houses contain many old books, which were passed on to them by their grandfather; they don't throw or give them away – it would be like throwing or giving away their grandfather. Nor do they use a feather duster to clean, it would be like feather dusting Grandfather. They do not buy new chairs, because this would mean participating in consumerist culture – a frivolity that would distract them from their studies, from reading. It is permissible, of course, to buy new books, and they do so with a mischievous gesture, as if they have just ducked out of their grandfather's lecture. They flaunt a new book as a Peronist would flaunt a new car.

Sometimes an inherited saying dances around in your head, one you have always hated. It's a reminder of the past, when young people would shed their coats in the first days of spring, and their elders would say, "Winter isn't done with us yet." You were annoyed because that comment seemed to wish for, to beckon the cold. But now you find yourself saying, "Winter isn't done with us yet."

TWO LADIES IN THEIR PLACE

THE ARTIST'S WIFE

He doesn't want her to be too pretty or made up (an obvious beauty would disrupt his creative work) or too ugly or unkempt. He hates seeing her clutch the broom vacantly, oblivious to her flyaway hairs – so he calls her Maritornes. He wants her to look just right, to have an appearance that offends no one. She shouldn't dress bourgeois, but more importantly, she should never come off poor. When she recycles outfits for work or literary gatherings she always accompanies him to, he feels as though she is reproaching him for not making enough money. She doesn't reproach him for anything: she teaches high schoolers. Once, all of her students stood up and pelted the blackboard with chalk. She didn't tell him about what happened. He would have reminded her that her family never learned how to set boundaries. Recently, she found a second job selling saucepans, but thank God she was able to fix things after the chalk incident because people don't want new saucepans – they use the ones they have. He didn't like the thought of her selling such things, it wasn't suitable work for the wife of a writer. If they had been books or paintings, well in that case…

She's not bothered about what she does for work. She'd have no problem being an inspector of hedges and sidewalks, a dog walker, a shopgirl. But she misses the conversations they had when they first met, about Kafka, Nietzche, and San Juan de la Cruz. Luckily, not all has been lost: he has two or three disciples who come by every other day. They drink up his words as eagerly as they down the coffee and pastries she gives them. She always forgets that the young bald guy drinks cup after cup of coffee and that the blond polishes off the pastries. So she has to go to the store before it closes, to pick up some more for the pair of them before tomorrow. What a shame: just when the conversation is taking an interesting turn, it's time for her to go down to the little corner store. He always reproaches her for going up and down the stairs a million times, instead of getting the groceries all together, in one trip. But since he doesn't participate in the day to day, the quotidian as he calls it, there are certain things he doesn't understand. She always hurries up the stairs, feeling as though she has missed something important. Even though she knows more or less what he's saying – and one must admit that he repeats himself at times – he always says it in a new way, with a new inflection, you know how it goes. And one day, if God wills it, or if her fate or the government improves, she will work less. Then the two of them will sit beside the fire (they will have a fireplace by then) and talk as they used to about Nietzche, Kafka, and San Juan de la Cruz, not to mention the new geniuses who will have come into the world by then.

GENERAL KNOWLEDGE

I'm here because I don't quite know how to express myself . . . My husband and son describe everything they see to a tee. My son studies architecture. They've formed a team. I've been left behind, on my own team. You tell me to write down what we talk about at dinner? Hell if I know, something about Maradona's pass. What if I write it down and forget the notebook, and my husband finds my notes? Sometimes he takes me with him and sometimes he doesn't, so who knows. Wait, he did promise to take me to Entre Ríos. Can we learn the names of the places on the route? You say "beltway" and I've heard this word on TV, but my husband uses other words to talk about the roads in Entre Ríos. Why don't we talk about something else since who's to know if he'll take me or not. I want to learn how to convert pesos into dollars. Oh, just like that, that's all? It's easy, lots of people must know how to do it. Yes, I like that story, where the loaf of bread tells us how it's baked. The loaf of bread can talk? Before I take the book home, could you check and see if it has drawings of snakes inside? If I see snakes, I run, I take off when I see them on TV, too. Have I been to any gatherings recently? Yes, I went to a wedding, but what is there to write about? You know how people are. Some are tall, short, bald, they dance. What else is there to write? I like that suggestion you gave me, just now. What did you call them? Little notes. Yes, one always needs to be reminded of something. I could send flowers and a little note that says, "Hope you have a great day." Inside the bouquet, or on the outside part? Sometimes I write to Vicente, the doorman, and say, "The keys to 4B are in 8H." Vicente with a "c" or an "s"? I really do like that thing about the little notes. I mean, if we set a price. Could I come every day? Oh, you have a lot of appointments, that's ok. Or if not, I'll leave it for my son, who comes home late from college, I'll leave him a little note on the table: "Son, take the steak out of the freezer and cook it in the big dish, it's in the oven." Bah, sometimes he doesn't even eat it, like when we returned from Spain. You ask me what I like. These days? I don't like anything. When I was young I really enjoyed swimming lessons and I also wanted to learn to drive, but never did. The truth is, I don't like anything these days.

MY TIME ON THE DIVAN

I'VE BEEN ANALYZED many times, individually and in groups. Twice I've gone to group therapy, first to a clinic in Belgrano where we took LSD to awaken our most dormant unconscious experiences. Then, the therapists began to study us. We had one session in a room with a fish tank – I remember the fish swimming outside of the tank, in the air. Among the participants was a fat woman who would always cry. She appeared before me as a woman from one of those Flemish paintings, with a bonnet on her head, her forehead swelling and shrinking. I also remember a young man who wanted to move around the clinic to be closer to the psychoanalysts, as if the clinic were a temple and he a worshipper.

When I was ready to leave treatment, one of the therapists said: "Going already, Hebe? It's worse out there." *Step off*, I thought to myself. And I left. A moment later I stumbled into an elevator with the head therapist and his assistant; they were leaving a floor where a costume party was going on, while I was going up to it. The two of them wore timid costumes: humble sheets and discreet crowns made from some little flowers or weeds they had picked along the way. I suppose they were dressed up as Roman consuls or proconsuls, but I don't know, it wasn't clear.

The second time I went to group therapy – a bigger group this time – we played a game where we encapsulated each other in a single phrase. One woman said that I seemed "godforsaken" to her. Later on I mentioned this to a friend who looked at me with intense sympathy. But the phrase hadn't left much of an impression on me – maybe because I thought God hadn't helped her out either. She was a secretary and pined after her boss, who would come and go as he pleased while she wondered whether he was really in love with her. I've never been fond of women who fall in love with their bosses.

As for individual therapy, I had my first session with a very good analyst. At first I didn't want to lie down on the divan; later, when I did, I leaned over to look at her. They say not to do this. In time, she progressed in her own way, fair and square, and went from wearing her hair in a small ponytail to styling it in an attractive way. She also moved into a new apartment, which got me thinking: "All of us patients contribute to her progress." I thought about it without resentment because I valued her very much; she deserved to progress – she'd been a great help to me.

There are two things I never understood about analysis, and the first has to do with February break. When February neared (I'm not sure why everyone goes on vacation during that month) and I was depressed or something like that, all of my analysts would say the same thing: "With February around the corner, we'll have to part ways." And I would think, "What does that have to do with anything? Who do you think you are?"

Another, trickier issue is that analysts have to build up their patients' sense of self. Since they cannot see their patients interacting in the real world, they excuse many things that they might otherwise find objectionable. For example, an analyst wouldn't say to a patient: "You're stingy." They might say: "You feel strapped for cash." Or let's suppose the patient is a thief or kleptomaniac, the analyst's interpretation tends to go like this: "He steals because he is unfulfilled."

All that aside, I think analysis is necessary at certain stages or moments in life.

IRAZUSTA

Once, when I did not have the money to go on vacation, I saw a TV ad for Irazusta, a town of a thousand residents. The reporter explained that the town was near Gualeguaychú and then asked some women cooking what kind of tourist attractions it had to offer. One of them said, "The handcar on the railroad and the otters bathing in the lagoon."

Not extraordinary attractions per se, but the women seemed optimistic about summoning a visitor. And so I went. I called a cab in Gualeguaychú and we rode along a hot, treeless road. When we arrived, the driver said incredulously "You intend to stay here?"

"Yes," I said in my most innocent voice.

The half a dozen dark houses in front of our cab did not have windows out front (to avoid direct hits from the sun). They looked like they were from around 1900. A woman was standing in the doorway of one of them.

"Buenos días, señora. Where in town might I spend the night?"

"Here in my home," the woman said.

"Would you like to see my documents?"

"No need, we know everyone here. But be careful with the dogs, they might follow you around – some of them are mooches."

With one glance, I took in the entire town. The houses were facing what used to be a train station. Now it was occupied by squatters, but it differed from the occupied houses of the city, which evoke a certain disorder and chaos. The station looked like yet another house, with its clothes, clean as can be, hanging on a clothesline. It fit in perfectly with the rest. From the houses and station, you could see the plaza in all its detail; there was a horse grazing beside the statue of San Martín. After dropping my bag off at the woman's house, I sat down on a bench in the plaza. I could see people coming from far away, as far as the sown sunflower fields; I could even make out the way they walked and the color of their clothes. Closer by, a slow and slightly hunchbacked boy was teasing a cow; he performed such long monologues that I was tempted to eavesdrop. I couldn't catch what he said. With my city wiles, I managed to get the woman who I was staying with to open up about the boy.

"Poor thing!" she said. "Not all there, is he?"

The house was dark inside, but comfortably cool, with TV, cable, and a telephone. It had really old furniture and my room – which belonged to some out-of-town son or daughter – featured a vintage television frame that had been converted into a bookshelf and beside it an ancient piece of furniture that had probably come from some German grandfather. My room did have a window in it, a low one the height of the bed. It gave me the feeling that the outdoors was at an arm's length. Every once in a while, a grunt from a nearby pig. A bible on the nightstand. I heard a cow mooing (others mooed in reply). It made me want to go outside to see what was going on. Going outside in Irazusta is not as it is in the city: once you get up, you are already outside. So it'd be possible to cover the town about thirty times a day, back and forth. The first things I saw were a plot of land, a cow, and a sheep. I paused to look at them. A man passing by said, "That's Rosa, the sheep is Mariana. Not from around here?"

"No," I said cautiously.

"Ah!" he said.

Later I discovered that everyone in town was in a frenzy because of this never-before-seen event – twenty tourists! All visiting because of a television ad. I told an architect from Gualeguay about it a few days later and she said to me, laughing, "Not in a million years did they imagine they'd see twenty tourists in Irazusta." But it was so. A sign with faded letters hung two steps from where I was sleeping. Written by hand, it said: *Library*. Then a girl ran out of the library, to the house where I was having breakfast, shouting, "A car, a tourist!"

I thought of the house next door as my breakfast spot, but it was also the spot where I chatted with the landlady, the two of us sitting together while people stopped by to ask for the price of student back-packs and folders. No one ever bought anything, but the landlady sent them off so kindly you would think they had just cleaned out her inventory. My cup of coffee was giant and the pastry came with sprinkles. She was an avid reader and had read a book about the history of Argentina.

"Pardon me," she said, "I don't know about you, but I'm not a fan of these modern books that say Belgrano could barely ride a horse or that San Martín took opium to keep fighting. I prefer the founding fathers as I studied them in sixth grade – we were taught that they were upright people."

I didn't think of contradicting her because I had more to see in town.

"Let's meet here again tomorrow," she said.

All the houses in town looked the same: they were all painted white, made from industrial materials, had small gardens in their front yards with decorations native to Irazusta, and open-air carports. Every carport was decorated with a floral arrangement. The only houses that stood out, just a touch, belonged to the history professor and the geography professor (who would serve dinner to us twenty tourists while her husband and daughter helped and her baby, who all of us played with, rolled around). Their houses were exactly like the others, except they didn't have a corral out back, or a chicken coop or pigs. I arrived at the history professor's house on foot. She was from the Uranga family, a distinguished lineage from Entre Ríos. She told me about the municipal government of Irazusta: instead of a mayor, they have a council they elect annually. Everything was perfect until it started to rain, and I wasn't able to leave. We continued to talk about this and that. At some point in the conversation, she asked:

"Do you believe in God?"

I figured that she did, so to stay on her wavelength (and because the rain was giving me cramps) I cooked up a theory about finding God in one's neighbor that landed fairly well. I was proud of myself, as if I had stitched together a delicate embroidery. What's more, I thought there's no way I'll be sent out into the rain and mud while we're on the subject of God. I would leave once it stopped raining. The sun was setting and the people who lived in the six houses facing the occupied and inactive station were taking their chairs out to the sidewalk. You could hear someone practicing the accordion.

I could have gone on reading in that little old room, but it was strange to read Barthes in a place where pigs were running around as they pleased. On the sidewalk, I might bump into some women who were expecting the pastor. They had bathed and dressed up their four kids (the girls in white socks) to wait for him. But the pastor never came. A mother with a freshly bathed baby in her arms said calmly, "He can't always make it, he's got other responsibilities…"

Without a fuss, life went on as though nothing had happened. I asked the grandmother if she knew someone who was up on the history of the town. It had to be some elderly settler, and someone who was still all there. She signaled to the house next door.

"Mr. Roque," she said, "he's home, why don't you go pay him a visit."

A woman who was chatting with her asked, "Didn't he go for the mare?"

"No, he already went this morning."

The houses were transparent. I went next door and Mr. Roque greeted me on the sidewalk, a true criollo with a bushy mustache, a handkerchief around his neck, and gaucho-style pants. His wife had a German last name; she was blonde and pale.

"Are you German?" I asked.

"Russian."

"You must come from the Germans that Catherine the Great took to the Volga River."

"Ah, who knows," she said.

Her origins did not seem to concern her. She had six children; three of them came out blond and three were dark-haired. Criollos (like the young man who came over and joined our conversation) stood out in their gaucho pants and little red scarves around their necks. The blonds (one was the owner of a neighboring shop) wore shorts, sandals, and graphic T-shirts. They later told me that Mr. Roque's son, the one who had chatted with us, was loitering because he didn't work. Mr. Roque filled me in:

"Our animals are very clever. The cows moo like crazy when something serious happens; they moo if they lose a calf or miscarry, and the others surround the mother gently. Animals who are bottle-fed" – a figure of speech, we say "orphans" – "are not to be slaughtered. The sheep and pigs in town follow people all the way to their kitchens. I had a horse who developed a taste for sugar. He would follow me to the kitchen, all the way to the cupboard. I learned how to bottle-feed baby colts, and that baby goats cry like children, and that sheep get cold when they give birth. I also got used to waiting for my cat, horse, and dogs by the gate. Horses should be broken tenderly; without tenderness, they rebel. All horses are not alike. I had a white one – clever thing – never got caught in the mancapotrillo weeds!"

He continued:

"Birds communicate danger to one another. First, the woodpecker gets excited and squawks like crazy to warn the mousebird, the shrewd mousebird hides in its nest, and the woodpecker warns the sparrow."

Since I couldn't keep all those creatures straight, I changed the subject to the hot topic in town: Yabrán, a powerful mafia boss, had committed suicide in Larroque, fifteen minutes from Irazusta. The whole country was up in arms because of the news and many theories were floating around.

"Did you hear that Yabrán died?" I said.

"That's what they say. God knows what happened."

Not a word more. He showed no interest, despite it having happened in a neighboring town. It was clear that Mr. Roque included Yabrán in his list of rarities, because the next thing he said was, "Two years ago a Dutch man came here straight from Holland. He visited me every evening, just like you, and asked me language questions. You should see how well he learned Spanish here in Irazusta! And he didn't come just once, he returned the year after."

I was astonished. How had he made it all the way here? How might his Spanish sound, now that he has an Irazusta accent? What a remarkable town. I promised Mr. Roque I would return, but I haven't yet. I still have my debt to repay.

KILOMETER EIGHTY-NINE

WHEN THE BUS MOVES slowly around the city, I feel as though I can get off at any moment to try some of "Grandpa's Medialunas," for example, or pet the little cat I see sitting on the balcony, or give in to that large sign outside a poor and hopeful shop that offers a gigantic ice cream with "Free Chocolate Glaze." But on the highway, it's full speed ahead. It's like we're on an airplane that has started to taxi. We're already gone. After a long ride, the pampas appear, but it's a "cosmeticized" pampas with pink flower trees at the side of the road. Nobody walks along the sidewalk; sidewalks don't exist there. All of a sudden, a large country villa appears, with swimming pools and a sign that says, "Ministry of Social Development." Then, some houses, dwarfed by towering highways, and finally a green countryside where the earth is dryer, but looks more natural, and I am reminded of those country complaints: "How awful! Green lawns during a drought!"

The first horses appear, grazing, and the pampas grass looks silver-plated. We approach Cañuelas, another cosmos of silver-plated plants, a few urban cows, an increase in cars. All of the cows are lying beside a tree and near them is the circular plaza of Cañuelas, where several women drink aperitifs under straw umbrellas. A sign: CAÑUELAS, THE LAND OF OPPORTUNITIES. More than opportunities, it seems like a land of varieties. Car dealerships beside a shop that sells charcoal – farther along, a warehouse with abandoned cars. The town seems provisional, as if it's about to shapeshift. Animals appear in the distance; the ones closer to the highway seem out of place, as though they had been sent away to a picnic. The ones in the distance are in their element. And how indecisive, that light blue in the sky.

JUAN PABLO AND CECILIA'S HOUSE

After driving along paved and dirt roads, we arrive at Cecilia and Juan Pablo's house. Their town used to be surrounded by dairy farms; some are still here, but not as many as before. In their place are summer houses. What to call these houses? Country houses? No. Farms? Not sure. They have vegetable gardens, but those are for family consumption, or rather, family pride: "This tomato came from my garden." In general, the houses are hidden behind trees or hedges, except for an old deserted bakery, more than a hundred years old, made of white bricks.

Its owner says, "I want to follow my late wife's wishes and turn it into a kindergarten or a museum."

"My wife was from there," he says, pointing to a field ahead of us that stretches toward the horizon.

The streets are dirt roads without names; to give directions they say, "next to the school" or "around the corner from Don Domingo."

Juan Pablo and Cecilia's house maintains a rugged air; millions of horn beetles are gathered around their door. Cecilia and Juan Pablo appear, along with Estanislao, their thirteen-year-old who they call "Esta," and Sibila, who is ten and spoiled. Esta tends to disappear. He goes off to play soccer and use the neighbor's kiddie pool, staying to eat because he was invited. That's how things go there: if someone has a pool, you take a dip, if someone's barbecued a lamb and has leftovers, you're offered a large portion without a second thought.

Cecilia tells me about her love for critters. "I've got an animal lover streak from my English side. When we used to look after grandma on her tall bed, the dogs would lie underneath; my uncle would bring his orphan lapwing to the house in Buenos Aires, another uncle had an armadillo, and my Aunt Margarita had a zoo."

I leaf through a booklet about her aunt's zoo; she used to buy animals at the Constitución bazaar and from rural areas, Paraguay, and Brazil. She'd inherited some money and sold jewelry to buy animals – an anteater, for example. (The good it did her.) She had seriemas who would confuse eggs with ping-pong balls and go off the deep end. A rhea, an armadillo that she put in a dirt-filled drawer so that he could dig holes, and the anteater, of course. A titi monkey who used to knock over flowerpots, another who was in love with a zookeeper – she would make faces all the time, to get his attention. Oh, and the rhea would drink water out of the kettle reserved for maté.

Cecilia has four horses. She says, "The one who talks to me most is Esperanza, she's treated badly by the other horses."

We touch on a few conversations relating to Buenos Aires, but none of them stick – they are like seeds the wind has blown to an unsuitable terrain. If some writer got married or divorced it ceases to be important when the cat is about to eat a dragonfly ("It has such pretty wings!") and you must go grab him. Or lead the horse out of wherever he's wandered into. "He knows he's not allowed in there," says Cecilia.

Just then, Sibila whines about a broken promise: she was supposed to receive a Ken doll, Barbie's country house, her dream house, along with a few of her other belongings. The complaint doesn't stick, Barbie and her accessories are so distant… Because Sara is on her way to visit, and she's taken a wrong turn. In this town, nobody gets upset about getting lost or retracing their steps. There is plenty of time. When she arrives, Sara is filled in on the transgressive horse, and it's clear she knows him because she says, "That horse is second-rate."

The animal who constantly receives the pinhead treatment is the dog they've brought from Buenos Aires. He gets too close to the horses, splays out in front of the car when he knows it's backing up, and is in a permanent frenzy about whatever it is he sees, which isn't negligible: cats, tiny birds, and loads of pretty things on the ground. The other dog, a local, seems calm, but he's rolled around in some animal bones – it's time to bathe him.

THE SEVEN TRADES

Even though Zapiola, where we're staying, is ten kilometers from Lobos and ninety from the capital, the town hasn't had electricity for long; they got it in 1985 or so, and the only telephone around back then was a crank phone at the general store. Today they have a makeshift first-aid station without a night crew. When it rains, it becomes difficult to transfer a patient to Lobos or call a doctor into town.

The general store has survived to this day, selling wine, soda, provisions, every type of boot, from rubber to leather, tall to short. The boots are in a separate room beside a pool table. Some lanky mannequins are there too, all dressed up. The crowd is a motley crew: countrymen wearing berets and boots, silently waiting their turn. People wearing shorts, lots of kids. Outside, sheltered from the sun, some little tables that are surely the center of the action. The whole family takes care of customers at full speed. With a calculator.

From the general store we go to Raúl González's house, which isn't easy to spot from the street – it's behind some dense hedges and has a small yard with a well-manicured lawn. Raúl González is a short, good-natured man who built his own house with bricks. The roof is low, the house reminds me of Snow White. Everything is tidy and clean.

Raúl says, "This whole area was dairy farms when I was a kid. My dad was a railroad worker and when it rained, he wasn't able to go back to town, so he would stay in Lobos. I was a railroad worker too, till the electricity came. Personally, I liked the steam engine, I would toss wood inside of it. See that photo? That's my dad with the station manager, he was very no-nonsense, an Englishman, he had some cows near the tracks and my dad used to milk them. When there was fog, they'd set off firecrackers as a warning and Dad would give us some to play with. My school was made entirely of wood, a shame they tore it down. Do you see those mosaics over there on the floor? They belonged to the school." The mosaics are perfectly matched to another area; so well, it seems the floor has always been that way. "We used to have fun at the barn dances – countrymen from the interior would come and dance the ranchera, polka, and a bit of pericón. When they left the dance, they'd go straight to work at the dairy farm. I built this house and both of my sons' houses, too. These ones."

He goes to find the photo of his sons and looks proud as he neatly stows away the salary receipt from his railroad days. After that, he shows me a photo of his mom – she's in another room, a room as tidy as the kitchen-dining area.

The entire room is covered in photos, the one of his mother is sepia and worn with time and the ones of his sons show them at parties, raising their glasses and sitting in folding chairs in the garden. His mom looks so serious in the photo, which makes me think about how people were more serious back then, and their lives more difficult.

As if reading my mind, he says, "Poor mama, she worked so hard. The way she kneaded bread! I got divorced around thirty-seven years ago and raised five kids on my own, all of them finished school and grew up to be teachers, shop owners, one a registered nurse. When I worked on the railroad, my sister would look after them for me, but you know how it goes, kids are always scraping themselves up, so I bought a small motorbike for myself, so I could make it home quicker from the train. When I retired, I took jobs in construction, I mowed lawns, did a bit of everything." The work seems to suit him: he's eighty-five, agile and content.

The biggest compliment you can pay another person in that place is to call them a hard worker. "A man of many talents!" they say. And that's because, even though the town is only ten kilometers from Lobos, which is a city, it's not possible to call a plumber or an electrician when there's an emergency. You must manage on your own, and that's why, in the same way that Cecilia Perkins collects cats, dogs, and horses, Sara Massini, the owner of the house where I slept, collects people who know how to do a little bit of everything.

She says, "I found Igor in Buenos Aires, his father's Russian and his mother Brazilian, he knew how to remodel furniture, install floors, and a thousand other things. His relationship with his wife fell apart, so he lived for a while in Villa 31. He was in the street for two years and I met him when he was eating in the dining hall of a parish. I brought him to Zapiola and he lived here for a while, but he used to get offended easily. He dressed a bit like a hippy, liked rock bands, and people here called him Charly, after Charly García. Not sure where he is now."

Sara no longer has Igor, but she does have a different guy who manages the electricity, plumbing, construction, gardening – she calls him Leonardo da Vinci. Leonardo da Vinci didn't want to talk about his life. "He has his days," says Sara.

And that's how life is there: a bad mood is like fog; one moment it's there, the next it's gone.

I slept in another house and was feeling guilty because the owner gave me her spacious bedroom so that I'd be right by the bathroom. She stayed in a smaller room, and a third one was occupied by her daughter's boyfriend's sound equipment. At some point, her daughter, the boyfriend, his friend, and an enormous white dog arrived. I woke up early, before anyone else.

Waking up first in city or country houses makes me feel sneaky – I don't know if I should make tea, or what. On the other hand, I was able to take my time and look at everything going on outside. More than look, I study everything.

Just then a thousand different birds were singing. I would have needed an expert to identify each bird with their song. One was laughing hysterically and another let out a series of thoughtful burps.

The dog of the house wouldn't let me take notes on the songs and their dispatchers because he was waiting for something: a pet, a massage, some attention. This humble white visitor knew his place and stood at a prudent distance, waiting his turn. The little cat also wanted something, but I realized then why cats are famous for their indifference: they don't bother you when they can't get their way. It's not that he was indifferent, but that he pretended to be.

At noon, we went to the general store and met Santiago Zabala, a horse-breaker.

We went outside to chat at the tables, and he was nervous about something, but it took him awhile to say why: "Sorry, it's just that my chicken's out there, and the dogs. . ."

He'd bought some chicken and left it at another table, so he got up, excusing himself. The thieves in this town are dogs. Zabala is of Basque descent, but he likes dressing like a gaucho; he wears boots, a beret, and a little red handkerchief around his neck. He's sitting tensely, as though waiting to take an exam. He says he's had many trades: fence builder, park landscaper, field manager, and horse-breaker. He traveled the world horse-breaking and has been to Roque Pérez, Jesús María, Tandil, Olavarría, Tapalqué, and Buenos Aires for the livestock shows.

He says, "I came up with a spectacle called 'Ready or Not.' Seven foals are let loose and the jockeys run in a swarm toward the horses to break them."

And he adds, "I named all my horses after birds." Oh, my bird expert! "I called them Sparrow, Thrush, and Canary. And I called my dog Gaby because of Gaby, Fofó, and Miliki, the clown trio. I had a pony that would spin around in circles like a dog and give me his hoof. And my small parrot would whistle and say, 'Ugly creature.'"

But the expert must leave, sadly, to cook his chicken! I would've spent three peaceful evenings asking him everything that came to mind.

He goes on, "When foxes catch the scent of a dog they scurry away with a yelp, but I've seen a fox make friends with a dog, and nobody believes me. I once caught two foxes, far away from my house, and one of them took the shackle off its mouth and left; no one believed me then either, that's why I photograph things now, so people believe me."

He takes out his cell phone and takes a picture of something.

RETURN

And with these sayings replaying in my mind: "Clodomiro Barrera, what a hard-working man, he died working," "When the horse smells a storm coming, straight to the fence it goes," I start to think: "Poor Clodomiro, poor horse," and the highway appears, with tons of cars zooming by in both directions.

"Will my bus come?"

"Yes, it will," my companions assure me. I always think that nothing's coming or going until it does. Soon the spirit of Buenos Aires appears: the bus fills up, nobody talks to anyone, everybody sleeps.

One girl, pretty and elegant, wearing bracelets up her bronzed arm, says to the driver, "Can you let me off at the Dropoff. . ."

"No drop-offs, only stops," the driver says.

"Oh, you're kidding me, they told me to meet them at the Dropoff. So, I" – emphasis on the *I* – "need to get off at the Dropoff! It's not possible it doesn't exist."

Patiently, the driver held his ground, but it seemed she wanted him to take us all to her imaginary drop-off. She got off reluctantly, without a thank you.

I DIDN'T KNOW

ONE SATURDAY, VERY EARLY in the morning, Javier, a history professor, Mirta, a doctor, and I left the city of Concepción del Uruguay (they call it "Uruguay," just like the country) to visit an indigenous community one hour and forty minutes away, in the town of Maciá. The town has around 8,000 inhabitants and a paved main street with one or two restaurants. Three blocks in, the roads become dirt and Mirta, who knows the lay of the land, takes us to the house of María Celia, a cacique. She is asleep because she spent the previous night taking care of an elderly woman who is ill. Seen from the outside, her house is spacious, new, and freshly painted.

We pay a visit to Luján, María Celia's daughter, instead. Luján used to work as a health-care agent in the Concepción del Uruguay hospital and Mirta wants to convince them to rehire her. But Luján doesn't want to go back.

"They discriminated against me," she says. "They'd send me – and no one else – out to the street to work. And what hurt most was when they fired me because, according to them, I'd been insubordinate toward one of my superiors. Since when?!"

An important clarification here. They are not insubordinate now, nor were they back then. Mass killings were carried out in the 19th century to rid them of their land; the final one happened in 1914. Back then, they didn't know how to write and were forced to surrender their lands with the mark of a finger – whoever refused was killed. But not only does Luján know how to sign her name, she also graduated high school and studied to become a paramedic. She is thirty or so, had her first son at sixteen, is pretty and sensible.

She says, "When I was in school, I remember noticing that everyone had Italian or Spanish backgrounds. I asked Mom where our family came from and she didn't want to tell me until I was old enough to understand, and when she finally told me about our indigenous roots, I was satisfied. The mystery was solved. My grandma was the one who'd pressured my mom to keep our indigenous origins a secret, because of the mass killings."

She adds, "In most history books it says that Columbus discovered America, but America was already here."

As we speak, her second husband Roberto Palomeque sits on the floor. He is quiet and smiling, polishing some tarnished pots until they are left gleaming. "I must revive them," he says.

I ask him if he went to school and he says no, but Luján says, "He reads everything he can get his hands on, high school textbooks, encyclopedias. He doesn't like soccer, though."

Luján holds a baby in her arms, breastfeeding her; meanwhile, three kids between four and nine years old are playing around us. I'd brought a few books with me, and I gave the oldest child *Jungle Tales* by Horacio Quiroga, the Latin American Andersen. Kids that age like *Jungle Tales*, regardless of their family's social class.

I tell the boy: "Ask your dad to read it to you."

"He's not my dad, he's my stepfather."

On our way out, Luján's eldest son, a high schooler of about fifteen, arrives on his bike. He is a bit chubby, a bit indifferent. He's got the face of a good student who's secretly a troublemaker.

I ask Luján, "Is he a good student?"

"Yes, he's good," she says evenly.

Roberto, the reader, affectionately picks up the baby (his daughter) and I ask Luján, "Where's Roberto from?"

"He doesn't know where he's from, he comes from the woods."

They laugh and Roberto, like wild buckwheat, accepts his uncertain origins in stride.

Their house is made of plastic, a kind of blue and pearl-gray igloo.

While Luján accompanies us to her mom's house, I ask why her mom's house is comfortable and hers is precarious.

She tells me, "I left the brick house to my first husband because I didn't want my kids to be raised in an environment full of tension."

MARÍA CELIA THE CACIQUE

María Celia, now awake, welcomes us into her spacious dining room. She has a pinewood cupboard and a large table with a map in front of it, a map that shows every indigenous group in the country. Below the map, a chalkboard and pointer.

She says, "The cacique is responsible for organizing the community, while the spokesman informs the members of new developments. We settle our problems in assembly, but when a controversy arises in the community, it's turned over to the council of elders."

It turns out to be something like a district court.

She adds, "A conflict arose because several of our brothers didn't want to be counted in the census. Some sociologists and anthropologists came to confirm that they were indigenous. The brothers claimed that they were pre-existing, so why should they be documented? Now we have eighty-six documented families and we're fighting over fourteen plots of land; there are thirteen clans, all of us intermingle and everyone knows each other.

My grandmother Victorina lived through the war of '14, the one in Europe and the one here. The registry began around that time. My grandmother raised me and forbade us from speaking of our indigenous background – she said they would kill us with their words, discriminate against us. And she was right, because things are more or less the same now: work is scarce, our women clean the streets of Maciá, and our men get by on short-term jobs. My grandmother and my great-grandmother used to work for a plate of food. My grandma Victorina was a very kind person, she'd tell us the story of the *solapa*, who is part woman, part eagle, and steals from kids during siesta time. She used to take all of us kids to the woods, to fish in the river. I worked in the woods as a logger; when we didn't have enough of something, my grandmother would say, 'Providence will save us' or 'The universe will give us strength.'

The land always gave us enough to eat – fruits, eggs – but we have no land left. If you go fishing in a stream, they'll shoot you down. The hunter's trail no longer exists – everything is enclosed in barbed wire. We used to have dogs who were bred to catch armadillos, others to catch otters. Standing, we were once able to see the thick woods. Stand up to see the thick woods, sit down and see the enemy. Now there is a project for a community vegetable garden and one for medicinal plants, but it's not the same, they don't fund us."

She tells me about the customs back then: "Men used to take their dogs hunting and they weren't allowed inside the house. To keep your dog from going inside, you'd cut a little piece of ear for him and bury it in front of the house, and you'd also bury your son's umbilical cord, so he wouldn't leave home. Mothers were allowed to hit their sons; fathers, no.

Women gave birth squatting down, clutching onto a tree. Even today, the ceremony of the first romantic encounter takes place by the river. The couples caress each other for the first time, starting with the feet, from the feet upward to the head, because the feet are in contact with the earth, where the strength is."

And she adds: "My clan was saved in one beheading because of a sick boy who found a hiding spot, while everyone else was killed – we are his descendants.

Later, she tells me, "I went to secondary school and then to community college and I wanted to go into business administration but couldn't. I really liked studying, I liked every subject except English. Later, I trained primary and secondary teachers."

María Celia the cacique wears a pendant representing the four stages (she explains that the fourth is sacred). The first stage is the one before the conquest, when natives inhabited the land; the second, the conquest itself; the third, the mass killings of the 19th century; and the fourth, the harmony between nature and man, which is still to come.

She says: "I represent Argentina in gatherings with other indigenous peoples and we are in contact with our Uruguayan brothers. When their lives were threatened in Uruguay, we helped them to cross the river, and they settled here."

She adds: "We are not a community, but a nation inside a bigger nation. Our name is Pueblo Nación Charrúa."

Later María Celia goes to the chalkboard and outlines the principles of the Charrúa nation. 1) Equality; 2) The Sacred Word; 3) Solidarity.

ALICIA

Neither Luján nor María Celia spoke of their private lives. María Celia is extremely cautious because of her role as cacique.

A round face peers in through a cracked window; later, the woman herself.

She says, "I'm Alicia, my identification number is 34225678, and I have more pelts on my body than words in my mind. I'm the daughter of Ñata Cuello; Los Andariegos played chamamé music with Ñata Cuello.

I had fifteen children: Griselda, Esmeralda, Dolores, Amilcar, Paola – some of my daughters are teachers. My mom named one of my children Juan Domingo, another María Eva, and I named one Alfonsino because it's thanks to Alfonsín that we live in a democracy. I separated from my husband José Dolores Díaz because he insulted me deeply; I was on my way to the Gutiérrez hospital in Buenos Aires to treat one of my disabled sons" – later she'll go to her house to show me a color portrait of her son – "and he told me that I was going to loaf around Buenos Aires. It was insulting, so I left him, though he was a very good husband. I loved my first boyfriend, Hugo Gutegal, and I never stopped loving him – where there was fire, ashes remain.

How did we get by? The village raised me. We lived in a hut with a palm roof, and later a thatch roof. We were a community, everyone took care of each other. Our neighbors, too. We sold wood. My mom didn't know how to write so she sent me to school. I was practically naked and barefoot, but I went anyway."

And she adds: "Now I go to the Catholic church, Evangelist too, and I don't believe in werewolves or evil light, but I do believe in Christ because he sacrificed his own life for our health, we are his guests here on earth. In my mind I see God seated, holding two staffs, one facing up and the other down."

Two little kids are sitting beside us, looking at some books with pictures of rabbits, pigs, and other creatures. Alicia looks at the books and says:

"Ay! Why do they illustrate animals that are going to be killed? Those are all going to be eaten – they should draw humans."

We couldn't visit a member of the council of elders because he was taking his siesta, so Mirta the doctor, Javier the history professor, María Celia the cacique, and I go to a barbeque. On the way, María Celia tells us about the assembly from the day before: the session had been cut short because a young man wanted to discuss politics, but the majority didn't want to. He'd also wanted to become a *taita* (a cacique) and they didn't allow it.

The barbeque spot is dark and long and run by an Italian couple – the wife runs the show. After announcing that she will not interrupt our conversation, she joins us at the table. She stays for as long as the food does, and relives an argument she had with a civil servant from the Maciá Municipality, concerning some administrative procedure. It's a cosmic diatribe, as if she were really talking to the civil servant and we were invisible. The hell with their papers, she told them, and the civil servant ordered fourteen inspections of the restaurant.

The cacique spoke measuredly about the plots of land that the thirteen tribes had demanded, adding at the end: "In the mayor's mind, being Indians means living in huts and wearing feathers."

So, the Italian woman says in a lively tone, "You need to fight harder!"

When we finish eating, the Italian woman gave the cacique the leftover meat.

The cacique said, "This is humiliating for me."

Did her reply have to do with the fact that her grandmother used to work for a plate of food – as she'd told us earlier? We explain to her that it's common in Buenos Aires for people to go home with leftovers. But it's possible the cacique won't get used to going to barbecues.

She adds, "I can't afford to make our situation tougher than it is – I don't look out for myself, I look out for my community."

And this prudent spirit reminded me of a criollo saying from the Buenos Aires province, for when someone calls out their adversary in a diplomatic way: "It seems to me, Roldán, that not all of these cows are yours."

Could it be that excessive fervor has no place in the universe? Or is it a fear of being oppressed, that criollo has borrowed from the natives? I don't know.

What I do know is, when we returned to Concepción del Uruguay, I told four different people that there was a Charrúa community in Maciá.

All of them said the same thing: "I've been to Maciá, but I didn't know about that community."

FABRICIO

I ONCE MET A MAN who belonged to space, not to time.
He believed that if he stayed in the same place for too
long he would deteriorate and shrink up. His name was Fabricio and
he always wore the same shirt, to "keep his clothes under control."
Coming up with new outfits takes time and he wanted to spend his
time moving from one place to another.

For example, he had devised a system to transport wood from the
north along the Paraná River. This seemed a much more efficient
means of transport than using trucks, which according to him were
"old, shitty, and slow."

"Who's there to claim the wood?" I would ask.

"Someone is always there," he'd say.

What he really wanted was to unite the people of the Paraná River
with those of Buenos Aires. What's more, he would harshly criticize
the farmers who lived north of the Paraná. They would bring a lot

of clothes and money when they visited the city (since, with money, anyone can travel). To him, traveling in such a way was ridiculous and ineffective.

"Those people may as well come with melons on their heads, that's how cautious and cowardly they are."

He said that fear would not exist in the future because people would travel with only the essentials in clothing, without money, or luggage, practically without a body. He had traveled from the countryside near Paraná to Buenos Aires, where he'd briefly stayed at a convent. He didn't attend the liturgy since it was too long a ceremony, so the nuns asked him to donate something, a colander, for example. But he believed that nuns should be dedicated to prayer. Why should they need material goods? They needed to be left alone with their things. So he moved in with an acquaintance who lived on the Uruguay River, for the time being.

Everything that pertained to residence was fleeting. Why tie yourself to one place? Once you understand its people and customs, it becomes an anchor, stranding you. What he really wanted was to collapse distance. It would have pleased him to see all the people of Buenos Aires living in Entre Ríos (for a spell, at least) and the other way around.

Quiet houses disheartened him; he wanted them to be remodeled in some drastic way, for some wall downstairs to be torn down. Details, repairs, painting, and cleanliness all seemed quedantista in spirit, anti-revolutionary. Why repair things just so everything can stay the same? Using a refrigerator as a desk, a curtain or bedspread as a little roof to block the sun, this is what interested him.

For instance, he used the flat surface of the refrigerator to make sailor's bread (he found the recipe in a nautical magazine he perused in his free time). Sailor's bread could last up to two years, invaluable sustenance for traveling the world. It is only possible to travel the world if one packs the minimum: instead of a coat, why not smear yourself with oil or tar?

He was a man of adventure and austerity. But, despite this, he had spent some money sending applications to England, to see if he might get into an English university even though he hadn't yet completed his engineering degree. He said he had never graduated because he'd studied in La Plata with some old, shitty notes. Also, everybody copied off each other. So he would go to England instead, to establish a routine, because the English all have tea and scones at five in the afternoon, unlike here, where everyone does what they want.

When he used to live in the countryside, he would tell the farmers that he had an account in a bank right beside the Plaza de Mayo.

He'd say, "Wait till I tell those nuns that I bank at the Plaza de Mayo with all those pigeons, all that power!"

One time he was refused credit at the bank (for floating logs along the river, or some other stunt) and he said, "I'm going to wake up before the pigeons and wait in line until the bank opens."

It seemed like an effective move for receiving credit, so why didn't they give it to him? Because despite occupying positions of power, they were narrow-minded and unable to see the future – they did not want progress. Sure, the bank was considered a sacred institution (for now), but for him, the most sacred thing was the moment when he baked a cake.

"The English have failed me," he would say, to sum up the experience. He eventually stopped thinking about the English and his world travels and concentrated on making dough. He would wait to put the dough in the oven and wait for it to come out, like a worshipper in a temple.

What he really wanted was to avoid the boring materiality of the world. According to him, it was not necessary to finish his first degree before moving on to graduate school; studies are slow and boring, as are teachers, houses, and trucks. What deserves to remain standing? The bank (for now), an oven for baking, and all kinds of surfaces made of all kinds of materials for making sailor's bread or other long-lasting edible substances. Keep in mind that the table must be multi-purpose: it could be turned into a divider, a raft, and in a pinch, a weapon of self-defense. All of this comes to mind because of an email I received from Fabricio, after not seeing or thinking about him for a long time, or knowing what had become of his life. The email says:

> If you are passionate about defending the environment and want to take
> part in a thrilling adventure to protect the Amazon, I am stationed at a

tent next to a gas station 200 km from San Pablo building tools from discarded steel found on the highway that leads to Mato Grosso, Peru, Venezuela, and Guayana.

Using a portable forge, I am making hundreds of tools according to a sustainable rainforest model which is part of the "Zero-waste industrial production" project.

We do not use petroleum, agrochemicals, or capital. We turn ball bearings into machetes, tire elastics into axes, and so on.

Perhaps the world of the future will be like that.

THIS IS A HUMANE COUNTRY

I WENT TO ASUNCIÓN BECAUSE I had a feeling I would like it. On the way to the hotel, the bus driver hit the brakes several times. During one of those halts, I landed straight on my backside.

"You have to hold on tight," she said, "Traffic's awful here."

Once I got to the hotel, a man visiting from the inland said to me, "Your Spanish is a little too good. We don't trust anybody who doesn't speak a bit of our local lingo because they might pull one over on us. Know what I mean?"

And yes, historically, they've dealt with many snakes in the grass – Porteño traders, and crooked Argentine and Brazilian lawyers. I began looking through some Asunción newspapers. In the Crime section, I found elaborate case descriptions. One was a sexual assault case led by female lawyers that lasted several days. On day one, a lawyer accuses her boss, a councilman, of sexual assault. (The woman appears in a giant photo.)

1. He asked her why she was so quiet and sad looking.

2. And said to her in Guaraní that he wanted to make love to her.

3. She asked that he show her respect (and in her testimony adds that he assaulted others who did not dare report him).

4. He made them sign a letter that said he was an honorable, respectful man.

The following day, the other lawyers step forward to report him. (Large photos of them accompany the text.) One declared that the councilman said he wanted to "eat her up" in Guaraní. She adds, "First he disappointed me professionally and then as a woman."

The third lawyer declared that her boss, now spiteful, called all of them "trash."

The councilman retaliates – he is allowed to reply in the newspaper – so there are accusations and counter accusations.

He says, "Ramírez is suspended because she crashed a car into her father-in-law's house."

A great number of people here crash into fences, columns, and private or enclosed stairways. In the same newspaper, it's said that a man has a restraining order against him, ordered not by his wife or ex-wife, but by the community hall. The accused is a mayor who they fear will go inside the offices to steal documents, gain influence, and take over the place by whatever means possible. In other words, it's to prevent him from destroying the community center. But the people who crash into those columns and buildings are "allegedly under the influence of alcohol." And why is "allegedly" added so often? Because being under the influence reduces your sentence by a lot.

I go for a walk around Asunción. The sun shines on the river and on the Casa de Gobierno, which is completely white. The police guards are playing music that aspires to be martial but sounds more like polka and chamamé. Despite the heat, I want to keep walking, so I go to the monument dedicated to the heroes of the War of the Triple Alliance. The Guazú War, as they say in Guaraní, the Great War. Looking over a railing, I spot an underground room. Inside is a monument for the child heroes, the ones who fought towards the end of the war disguised as elderly people. A guard sees me looking down there and says, "You've cast down your eyes to signal submission."

Huh? Me, signaling submission? I didn't ask him what he meant. Walking, farther, farther, I got to a bookstore where I spotted a book called *In Search of the Lost Bone*, a reference to Proust. The allusion to bones has to do with what General Francia said about Paraguayans: they are missing the bone that keeps their heads upright when they speak to someone.

The book has nine editions, published between 1990 and 2000. Helio Vera, the author of this treatise on Paraguayology, is eager to identify the defects of Paraguayans and denigrates them for their corruption, cronyism, and short-sightedness. His self-deprecation saddens me. Could being so unforgiving lead to change, or will the reader become paralyzed in the face of a sad, predetermined destiny? I don't know.

And yes, they do believe in liquid courage. St. Onuphrius is the patron of drunks; he protects them from getting beat up on their way home. How do they square this submission with such exacerbated individualism? At the very least, it's certain that their wills are strengthened by their wild imaginations. It's also related to deficient institutions. According to Vera's Paraguayology treatise, one president went to bed elected and woke up removed from office. Everything must happen right away, right now, before one's plans are thwarted.

I read in the newspaper: "Kiara and Andrómeda, twin psychics of the highest caliber. We unlock forbidden and impossible loves in seven hours. Other facilitations: divorces and joint inheritances – all without having to leave your house!"

And who wouldn't like everything to be quick, easy as magic? Other names are just as capricious and strange as the twins' – one fortune teller is called Mesalina.

An ad for eggs called "Nutrihuevos." They are simply eggs, but the compound word gives them more power.

Paraguayans also attribute power to light, to the shimmer of gold. One jewelry shop is called Radiance. Often, flower wreaths for the dead are also lit up. Since radiance bewitches, women want to be radiant, which is why they wear gold T-shirts, carry gold purses, and keep gold in their imagination. Gold evokes dreams, just like the fur capes they sometimes wear with their wedding dresses. In this case, it's a dream of snow.

One dance club is decorated with giant panthers and lions in a vivid green forest – the mural covers the entire wall. It's a dream of the nearby rainforest. The countryside is also nearby, and this can be heard in the way people speak. Personally, I like it.

The controlling part of me says, "They don't distinguish between public and private."

But, in practice, all I need to know when I'm getting dressed for the day is that it's going to be as hot as "la gran flauta." I read in the newspaper that a soccer match was "postponed due to a wasp invasion." Yes, a slice of the country inside the city. And between ads for sound equipment, ice cream makers, glass cutting machines: "Male Ostrich For Sale," "Fertile Buffalo For Sale," and the perfect ad: "I Buy Anything."

The memory of Asunción always returns when I come across the poet and anthropologist Amaral. He invited me to his tidy apartment, which was comfortable, nothing flashy. He was an old man and sat on his sofa looking dignified in his pajamas. He told me that his ancestors, dating back to 1700, came from both Buenos Aires and Paraguay. But he had decided to live in Asunción. It wasn't exactly balmy outside, and a young cleaning woman was opening all the windows.

He asked her, very gently, to shut them and told me, "She always likes to have a breeze, even when it's chilly. Do you know why? Because she comes from a nomadic people."

I've never heard a more respectful and thoughtful explanation. Inwardly, I compared his reply to what we would have said in Río de la Plata.

"May I ask why you don't live in Buenos Aires?"

He said, "Because this is a humane country. The 18th, 19th, and 20th centuries co-exist here."

And he explained what I had seen in the city center, the cybercafe and the "cibercocido" (where you can use a computer while drinking maté cocido made with herbs that were sold by the women sitting in the plaza). And he told me about the young people downtown, with their cell phones and trendy city clothes. He had fallen in love with Paraguay. I had too.

AROUND THE CORNER

A FEW DAYS HAD GONE BY since my arrival in Cartagena (or "Carta'ena," as the young waitress called it)
and I had already observed all of the diners at the hotel restaurant.
Several loud Mexicans who knew how to enjoy life, and many, many
Argentines who did not view life as a pleasure, as the Mexicans did,
but a duty.

"The weather shouldn't be this humid."

"They say that the weather is just right in Santa Marta."

"The food should be less salty and they shouldn't let the mariam-
ulata" (a fat and squat moocher of a bird) "eat off the floor. It's not
right for a hotel of this caliber."

The restaurant was outside, overlooking the sea, and there was a
tree in the middle of the dining area. Two pairs of newlyweds (or so
they seemed) were there, too – one Argentine and the other Chilean.

At first glance, they were very similar – the men's clothes were identical. The men themselves were identical, the girls not so much. The Argentine girl had arranged her hair in an effortless hairstyle, and showed off a sliver of midriff as if it were something demanded of her, a princess; as if she left no detail up to chance and at the same time wanted to give the impression that everything was improvised.

When I told the waitress that she was from Argentina, she said, "Really, Argentina? I don't believe it, Argentines are so…"

"So what?"

"They complain about every little thing."

But the diner who stuck out the most was a drunk Englishman. He had already had (several) pints by breakfast and sat there as if stranded; it was apparent that he didn't have any excursions planned, not even to the beach which was right there. And he didn't intend to visit the old town either, because he'd already seen it in a previous life. He seemed to be traveling the world chained to hotel restaurants and bars, as if the world were just an old house he knew inside and out, unworthy of even the slightest glance.

I'd hardly leave the hotel and cross the street when twelve or so street vendors (who were forbidden to loiter on the hotel sidewalk) would begin following me, all of them black or mixed, men and women. I'd buy something from them so they would leave.

They'd say: "Friend, sister, where you from, huh?" and they

wouldn't leave me in peace, not even at the little bar where I went to read. One of them, Rosa, wanted to paint my toenails.

She'd say, "Those feet have worked hard enough. Let Rosa take care of your feet."

"Tomorrow," I'd say.

The next day, in the middle of the street, Rosa painted my toenails blue. I sat against a felled tree and she kneeled. Four tall men selling necklaces and watches stood around us, watching. It felt like something out of a dream. When she finished the operation, all of them lingered behind me.

I sat down to read and announced, "I'm not buying anything today."

They protested.

"Buy something from him, he's an old man…"

"I'm not buying anything today because I'm sad."

Miraculously, it worked.

As the old man went on protesting, another member of the group said, "Can't you see that she's sad?"

And they left.

I didn't want to go see García Márquez's house, I had already gone to the old town every day, walking about twenty blocks; I'd seen people dancing in the plaza and every gringo in the universe sitting in their chairs, riding in carriages. I'd explored every nook and cranny of the old town. Just then I heard two Argentines talking in the hotel lobby: they were planning to go to Santa Marta. I joined in on their conversation; apparently you had to take a plane to get to Santa Marta, where the water is clear, as it should be, and the landscape is just right, the sea foam too.

I didn't have money or the desire to board a plane that would take me far away, and I thought: "Everyone's going so far away, on such long excursions. I should go somewhere too, but just around the corner. I'm one for coastal travel."

Beside the large pier was a smaller and more precarious one. I liked that – since it was smaller, I thought it would be easier to board, no lines or anything. A man selling tickets from a sort of shed told me to get a roundtrip ticket.

I said, "And when's the return?"

"Ask Cal-los once you're there."

It wasn't indicated if the trip would last one or five hours. But the vendor was an amateur, he sidestepped my questions. I got on a little boat that was as worn out as my feet. All of the passengers were poor and black, except for one girl, who seemed a little better off and sat dreamily at the bow, alone, thinking about some love of hers. The boat rocked back and forth, it was going at full speed though it seemed to be pedal-operated; the captain walked among all the seated passengers. Nobody seemed alarmed, so I wasn't either. When we finally arrived, three necklace vendors were waiting for me at the dock. How often did tourists visit? Who would've gone there? Maybe some official visited once and was persuaded to buy a necklace. I started to explore the little island, three necklace vendors trailing behind me; they were more reserved than the ones in Cartagena.

When they saw me, they must have thought, *Things are looking up.*

The houses there weren't surrounded by any trees, the ones in the distance were rickety. Little white plastic chairs and a hen inside an abandoned chapel. The cemetery was overgrown with weeds and everything was in plain sight: kids, dogs, people busying themselves inside their houses. I told the necklace vendors that I wanted to walk alone for a while and immediately regretted it. The sun stung so sharply that if I left them behind, I wouldn't be able to seek shelter in their shadows. One of them should sell hats . . .

The houses were built out of a strange material, they had very thick walls painted yellow, white, and green. Every movement on the island gave it the air of a shantytown – the circulation of dogs, pigs, and children – but the houses didn't seem like shanty houses, they were more like miniature fortresses, from a time long ago. The yellow of the walls had taken on a camel color.

I asked a quick-witted looking man if there were any ruins around. I had already come to the last of the houses. He whistled and a serious, polite young man came immediately, from far away. Without a second thought, he led me through the grass to another camel-colored building – it was an abandoned fort nearly covered with weeds. In the 18th century, it had been a Spanish watchtower for pirates. The boy told me where the Spaniards used to store their cannons, among other things. Then I looked toward a deep trench and the boy said that they used to fill trenches like that with reptiles.

And he added, "The Spaniards would throw slaves who behaved badly in there."

What did they consider bad behavior? What about the boy – what did he think about this? If he had something on his mind, he didn't say it, but I thought about how a crocodile might have eaten one of his ancestors in there. I couldn't stop thinking about it.

I could tell he was intelligent – he spoke eloquently – and I said, "You should be in school."

"I had to drop out, I work now."

From that point on I took on the role of counselor; I gave him a ton of advice about studying, about work and life. Then he took me on another tour and the three necklace vendors joined us along the way, as though they'd been waiting for me, and we went to a shed. The shed had a thatched roof and looked modern and sophisticated next to the little houses from the 18th century; in the center of the dirt floor stood a long table. Some little creature was being cooked on a grill. I ordered a Coke and within two minutes the young guide, the necklace vendors, the woman who owned the place and a man from around there sat down beside me. I offered them some Coke and we got to chatting.

In a local accent, the man asked, "Where you from?"

"Buenos Aires."

Yes, I was from Buenos Aires. And in that moment I felt like a pollster, traveler, and teacher all at once because I asked a lot of questions. They were grateful to President Pastrana because he had brought them electricity a little while ago; meanwhile, their water was not potable.

And, in the voice of a teacher, a revolutionary even, I said, "But you should have potable water, the weeds shouldn't be so overgrown in the cemetery, you should –"

The man said, "How sweet it must be to travel!"

Without a moment's hesitation, I said, "But you could travel if you'd like, just like me. You could board a ship and see the world."

Enthusiastic by the idea of him traveling, I thought, *He should travel*, but I didn't say this to him.

The man replied bitterly, "Back then we could, but now, nobody wants to let us on their ships. Once they know we're Colombians, that's that."

I caught a glimpse of his frustration – the world was full of impossible things – but the counselor in me prevailed.

I turned to the necklace vendors and said, "And you gentlemen could sell necklaces in Cartagena! People sell a lot of things there."

"We're not allowed. You need a permit there, and that's real pricey."

Selling necklaces in Cartagena was an unattainable dream reserved for tycoons. It was a setback but I didn't give up.

I said to my improvised guide, "And you have to go back to school."

Using the others as witnesses, as though making a pact, I said, "He has to go back to school."

Dead silence and a withered expression on the mature young man – his eyes became gloomy, irritated. At that point I realized that my role as teacher had come to an end. The sun was scorching the ground and I wanted to go back to Cartagena. The necklace vendors walked back with me to the dock. I bought a necklace from each of them, but they kept walking and chatting with me after the sale. We talked about this and that.

Luckily, a boat similar to the one that had brought me there was leaving. When we got about ten meters away from the coast, an eight or nine-year-old boy, who was using a piece of styrofoam as a table, came up to the boat to ask for change. I didn't have one coin, or any sweets or cookies. Only necklaces and large bills.

"What can I give him?" I thought. "I know: a necklace."

And I gave him one of the necklaces I had just bought.

He should have cursed me out; I would've done that if I were him.

THE LAND OF FORMOSA

O N T H E D A Y O F my arrival, I walked thirty or so
blocks to the port. Formosa is on the Paraguay River,
a calm grayish river whose stillness encompasses small barges and
a large freighter topped with shipping containers. It looks like a
homestead floating on the river, and the statue on the banks, posed
as a colonizer, is a natural addition to the group. Two women beside
me are speaking in Guaraní, laughing easily.

"I didn't catch any of that," I say.

"Better off," they tell me. "It's very crude."

Confronted by so much space, so many forking paths, one has the
desire to go everywhere. The river splits into two streams and the
bordering road into two routes: one leads to the hotel and the other
to the Paraguayan market.

I find a seat on the terrace of the large tourist hotel and buy a
newspaper. I only manage to read the literary supplement written by

readers of the paper. One person has written an ode to his eyeglasses, praising their usefulness. The final line: "Little lens, I love you so!" A celebratory and grateful spirit abounds. Children's birthdays are announced with captions such as "Thank you for being born, sweet little queen" and "Our lives were drenched in sunlight when you were born."

The space in front of me is as ample as the time that passes before the waiter brings a coffee. My newspaper is swept away by the north wind in half a second; it's time to go to the indigenous craft fair by the river. The crafts are pale and lightweight, evoking the cleanliness of the people who live there. Spoons and utensils carved from pale wood, freshly woven rope baskets, beautiful skirts made of vegetable fibers.

Beside this fair is another one, known by the name "Made by Paraguayans" (Paraguayans are omnipresent, as if they are relatives of the Formosans; many of them come from Alberdi, which is fifteen minutes away by speedboat). Compared to the light-colored crafts of the indigenous fair, these crafts are dark and somber, reminiscent of the old market in Luque, Paraguay, where one is reminded of the many generations that have shopped under its cool canopies. Loud cumbia music plays, and all kinds of things are for sale, including a gigantic felt Yacaré caiman. Nearby, there is a grocery store called M'barete – "powerful" in Guaraní.

The Lampagua bookstore is a block and half from the riverbank.

It's small and bustling. Braulio Sandoval, the owner, is a historian, poet, professor, printmaker, one-man band, and compulsive greeter, like the lapwing. He meets me outside, where the sidewalk meets the street. Sitting in two little chairs facing each other, he explains that Formosa was late in separating from Chaco; it happened in 1879. Only recently, in 1955, was it declared a province. It took some time for its constitution to be drawn up. He mentions that the territory isn't known for its famous last names and that its first settlers were Italian, Spanish, and Paraguayan immigrants who later became ranchers. It's a multi-racial place. A brief historical explanation, a little greeting to a passerby, and a tour around the bookstore to see how things work.

"There go two dancers," he says. (They stop and chat with him.)

"I'm distracted," a journalist says to them.

I don't know whether to interview the dancers about the agricultural boom, or ask Braulio Sandoval – given the frequency of his greetings – if there's anyone in town he doesn't know. He ducks into the bookstore and I lose track of him, but he leaves me with a friend who tells me useful historical information and has the advantage of being a still man.

. . . . . .

Lot 68, located eleven miles from the city, is home today to a community of Toba. It has a large, well-built school complete with a kindergarten. I wanted to see a bilingual class taught by Toba teachers; they also have "memas," locals who act as interpreters and, at the same time, preservationists of the language. But the principal didn't let me come inside because I wasn't authorized; she suggested I go back to Formosa to seek authorization. I asked if she had the names of any of the old settlers who might know the history of the place, but apparently no one was available.

The cab driver who had dropped me off clarified the situation: "The problem is many visitors have said ugly things about Formosa."

I was carrying a bag with pants, t-shirts, books for the teachers and kids (Jungle Tales by Horacio Quiroga, which I had purchased at the Lampagua bookstore) and because of some hidden corner of my personality that pushes me to bestow gifts on those who punish me, I left the contents of the bag with the standoffish principal. A wrinkled bag in my hands, unsure of where to go next, the photographer and I went to talk to the memas who were standing outside. One of them, Walter, was tall and sturdy as a tower. When he talks to the kids in Toba, they say, "You don't talk right," because their parents wanted them to be taught Spanish.

"But recently," he says, "people have started to raise awareness and are more in touch with their roots."

They gave me the name of an older settler, Señora Teresa, and a young man showed us the way to her house. All of the houses we saw were made from industrial materials; one had reggaeton music coming from it.

"Do you like reggae?" I ask the young man.

"No, I'm more into cumbia villera."

We arrive at Teresa Rivero's house, made from the same materials, a little rundown. She used to oversee a student cafeteria. As gentle as can be, she places three chairs on the dirt patio.

She says, "My husband's name is García Raúl and I'm Rivero Teresa." (The reversal of names must be because first names are used for business.) "I was trained in mediation. For example, I used to accompany elders who didn't know Spanish to the capital to run all of their errands. My daughter specializes in teaching native students." She glances toward the house and says something softly in Toba. "I left Pirané at fifteen and never returned. Back home, we would eat fried ñandú, grilled, too, and we had plenty of honey. When I first got here, everyone was living in shelters made of palm trees and cardboard and my husband García Raúl built a house using industrial materials. We were the first to do so – my husband was a bricklayer. I guess the mayor was embarrassed by the shacks, which could be spotted from the main road, so they began to build every house with bricks. I've always worked at the clinic, the cafeteria, and you know, we've never had enough medicine and we don't have our own ambulance."

She goes inside and gives instructions in Toba.

"What worries me is the new generation. They are losing their culture, there's too much alcohol, inhalants too. It all starts at the soccer field; they pool their coins together and start drinking. We never knew what it was like to bail a kid out of jail – it was white people who introduced them to drugs."

I gave her all I had, the frayed and empty bag, and Teresa Rivero gave me a shiny new basket made of glass.

THE UNIVERSITY

The following day, I visited the public university. They were in the middle of a political campaign to elect delegates and student union leaders. Music was playing through the loudspeaker – it reminded me of Ricky Maravilla.

The lyrics went like this: "The elections are here, I vote, I vote happily." Afterward, on the loudspeaker, "Together we can make a difference."

The dean gives me a warm welcome and sends me to Professor Mirta Pubiano, who is interested in the subject of bilingual pedagogy and tells me about the indigenous students who attend the university.

"We failed them in the beginning. We didn't consider their specific worldview, so we didn't get the results we wanted. Things got better once we consulted an anthropologist. For example, university instructors tend to specialize in one area, while the instructors of indigenous communities are more general, they teach all facets of life. It was difficult for students from indigenous high schools to understand the phrase, 'The tree is in the garden,' because to them, trees belong in the forest." She adds: "We didn't understand certain behaviors. For example, we wanted everyone in a group to speak up, not just one person. But for them, it was just the opposite: they are used to having a spokesperson. It's also worth noting that, among the Toba, grandparents are more important than parents." The professor invited me back the next day. This was when I spoke with two literature students; one of them, Víctor, was ethnically Toba. Víctor wrote poetry in both Spanish and Toba, with epigraphs by Aristotle and Sartre. He hesitated for a while before sharing his writing with me, observing me with his large dark eyes while he rustled around in his backpack, as if he were buying himself more time.

He told me that he had kept a diary since he was eleven, but had stopped doing so recently: "I'm so disorganized," he said, smiling for the first time. His greatest influences were his grandmother's stories and his move to the city. He didn't have the diary, but the professor gave me an open letter to read, written by Wichi students in 2003.

They wrote many things, including the following: "During the first days of class, we were panicked by the academic standards, which were very new to us. Many things are still difficult for us to understand. This happens on a daily basis, like when professors arrive late to class and leave early, or when they lecture nonstop, and nobody interrupts because we are afraid of making them angry. They only expect questions from select students and we tend to sit in the back of the classroom by ourselves, isolated."

The other boy, Nicolás, gave me an anthology of stories and poems that his work had appeared in; he sang Professor Mirta's praises and accompanied me to the bus terminal, which was near the university.

THE CATHEDRAL

The cathedral is spacious, as everything else in this city is; inside are very few images, an altar with a simple, floral cloth and a homily chair made from what looks like palo santo. The unpolished wood gives off a rustic air, as do the little balconies whose railings remind me of a hotel patio – all of it signals the pioneers' desire to have at any cost and as quickly as possible, their own cathedral. A painting of the Virgin Mary and her child hangs in one of the wings; both have present-day features. On the street, I notice another mural that depicts Mary holding baby Jesus, who looks like he could just as easily appear in an advertisement for diapers or oats. A beam of light, pink on one side and sky-blue on the other, shines on the figure of Jesus. Worshippers offer a serenade to the Virgin Mary (they also serenade her during birthdays and other celebrations), and I find out that the bishop has written a version of the Stations of the Cross that is "the longest in the world." The Stations of the Cross appears in every apartment in Formosa; each station is dedicated to a distinct part of society (natives, pioneers, missionaries, etc.), and each text reads like a short historical synopsis. Formosa's history recalls blood, sweat, and tears, the immeasurable difficulties of cutting mountains and building the railroad. The Stations of the Cross also points out the abuse suffered by natives.

I interview Monsignor Scozzina, the bishop who wrote this Stations of the Cross. He is a wary old man with piercing eyes. I mention what I've seen and learned about the city: changes from the past ten years, fresh concrete, construction plans, and the hospital complex. A little overexcited and frivolous, I want to know more about the serenades for the Virgin Mary (I can't bring myself to ask him about serenades in general, although I'd like to). In the end, I say that the city seems to be flourishing.

He fixes his eyes on me and says, "But there's so much poverty once you go inland."

THE IMAGINARY

I try to learn more about the Formosans through their murals and sculptures. Right away these seem remarkable for their blend of religion, patriotism, and nature. One mural at the port depicts a procession with the Virgin Mary on a platform wearing a halo – a striking, brown, inverted cone. Above the halo is a cross and, behind the procession, some kind of establishment that says "Kiosk." Mary wears the Argentine flag as a sash.

I see a group of sculptures in front of the courthouse, including Laureano Maradona and a mother embracing her children. Maradona was a selfless doctor, adored by the natives. He was also a teacher and naturalist. He arrived in Formosa one day, just passing through, and he ended up staying for fifty years. The size of Maradona is gigantic compared to that of the mother – he is a titan. It seems that Formosans represent the world as a latent potential. Maradona's massive size encompasses his extraordinary social work, just as the gigantic toy caimans on sale encompass the forces of nature. A plaque above me reads: "El dotor Dios," or "Doctor God," what the natives used to call him.

The prison is right in the center of the city, with a curious cluster of sculptures out front: an enormous, mauve-colored globe with Latin America painted a bright yellow and an enormous serpent circling it; farther up, an evil looking figure, and an eagle presiding over everything. I ask passersby what it could mean or what the authors may have wanted to express. Nobody knows, but a prison guard says: "They say it's the Apocalypse." Luckily, nobody is disturbed by its arrival.

Some literature students at the public university published an anthology of stories and poems. It's called *Alquímico*. They dedicated it first to God and then to nearly a full page of names. In addition to its literary value (included are quotes from Borges, Lorca, and St. Augustine, among others) the texts reveal a worldview in which nature is perceived as violent and in motion. I quote: "A bare neck feels the caress of the Earth's creaking hinges;" "The music of the sun crescendos;" "A tower rises like an arrow and is nailed to God's forehead;" and "In every trace of this naked north, this land of dirt and blood."

Another text is directly tied to the Stations of the Cross. Dirt, blood, and endless sacrifices, just like the ones the bishop mentions in his version, dedicated to the department of transportation, to the workers who time and again replace the river embankments destroyed by floods. Here nature creates an epic that makes it impossible to forget the formidability of its forces. It results in a cross between Prometheus (Dr. Maradona), the cleaning of King Augeas's stables, and the myth of Sisyphus. Man creates and natural forces destroy.

Nicolás Gómez, whose writing was included in the anthology, wrote me a memorable dedication: "To Hebe: may hundreds of archangels lift you beneath your wings, so that you may enjoy the birds of the night sky, the sound of "the unspoken" and the eternal redemption that faith has in store for us."

I visited the animal sanctuaries near the city; one of them had big colorful parrots, so-called "pocket monkeys," and a Brazilian species known as a "finger monkey," named for their tininess and bristly white hair that makes them look angry. In the sanctuary's habitat, Yacaré caimans might be spotted at sunrise – I hear it mentioned that caimans are eaten in milanesas and used as empanada filling. I also visited the radio station Pinocho FM. Sergio Domínguez, a historian, comes on the air in the morning. Formosans always seem to be in a rush, multitasking, and I wanted to get to know them better.

Sergio said proudly, "We are multicultural, multiethnic, and multilingual. We're a hopeful society – we believe that good things are coming. We've always kept our gates open, trusting the goodwill of those who pass through them." (A digression: nobody opened the gate for me. My point of contact for interviews vanished and I never heard from her again – she didn't even bother making up a white lie.) Mr. Sergio went on, "We know how to let time pass, how to let things run their course. We believe in what we can give to our province, not what she can give to us."

In the past ten years, Formosa has flourished more than it has in the fifty years prior. There's no denying it: they have housing plans, a lot of fresh concrete, and a sophisticated new hospital complex that fills them with pride.

Mr. Sergio says, "The people of Formosa enthrall me, their prudence – the Formosan is a man of few words."

Concerning the restraint and patience of the Formosan man, I've heard other opinions. Pinocho, the head of the station, confirms what the historian says about the good qualities of the city: "You can always find me here, in the San Miguel neighborhood. It's a Republic: great singers and soccer players had their start here; we think of it as a slice of heaven on earth."

I ask him where one might go to listen to a serenade and he deflects the question: "The serenade is a state of the soul," he says. He adds: "We do not deliver bad news, only good. We talk about the airplane that lands, not the one that crashes . . . We don't play cumbia villera because it encourages drug use. We play Paraguayan music. The Paraguayan singer evokes the impossible – he sings to the valley his lover leaves in the pillow."

I felt deflated by the part about the valley in the pillow because I hadn't managed to have coffee with anyone in Formosa or listen to a serenade. I wanted to leave early, but I still had something left to do: track down a study by a Formosan sociologist or a compilation of local idioms, something written by the Formosans themselves. During my walk I stumbled upon a neighborhood with a good book-store, La Paz. I asked if they carried the study and no, they didn't, but I did find a magnificent collection of O'Henry stories. O'Henry is one of the most delightful writers, and to find him in Formosa after having looked for him for so long in Buenos Aires seemed like a stroke of luck. He is the kind of writer who believes in the tricks fate throws our way. Satisfied, and wanting to say goodbye to someone, I went to the port to visit the owner of the Lampagua bookstore, the one I'd talked to on my first day. I told him some stories:

"I went to the Guaycolé sanctuary."

"Mhm."

"I went to Lot 68, to visit the Toba."

"I heard."

"How did you hear?"

He gave a quick and muffled reply while he handled a few things in the store. How did it get back to him, in a city of 200,000 inhabitants?

At the airport, waiting on my delayed flight, I go outside and take a stroll along the sidewalk.

A man approaches me immediately and without preamble says, "Excuse me. Will this be your only visit, or do you have plans to return to Formosa in the future?"

I take it he wants to know why I came in the first place.

"Just visiting," I tell him. And with my most innocent face, I talk about the number of motorbikes I saw in the city, the little birds at the wildlife sanctuary, and how cold it got. Soon after I boarded the plane.

RÍO IS A STATE OF MIND

T HE PAULISTA POET Mario de Andrade, inspired by the Río de Janeiro carnival, wrote these lines:

> Heroic longing in my senses
> to uncover the secret of beings and things,
> I am the beat that unites every other beat,
> I dance in multicolored poems.

Everything in Río is colorful and over the top. The streets are full of people, full of disparate activities and noise. It's clear that the noise doesn't bother Cariocas because they have happily imported a device that heightens the intensity of sounds, to hear better and louder. Río is a chorus that belts out a little bit of everything. One postcard has ten toucans on it (the toucan often appears as a decorative motif and rivals the falcon in terms of political symbolism) and all ten of the little birds are perched on a traffic light post.

While throngs head to the beach, others weave through the street with baskets, rods, packages. Cars charge ahead and people tend to cross the street running. In the central plaza, the only sharply defined details on the monument for General Osorio are the general and his horse; below them, a shapeless mass of hazy soldiers, dead, alive, injured. It reminds me of Spinoza: some live, while others die; some rise, while others go to sleep – every variety of existence does nothing more than reflect the unity of nature. In Río, you feel intensely . . . between the bodies, the heat, the beach, the dancing, the huddles of people watching capoeira performers downtown, all of it creates the sensation that you are an active part of the whole, part of the collective body.

Clarice Lispector echoes this intensity of life. She says: "I am not going to be autobiographical. I want to be *bio*." To face the force of that sea, of those hills, that beauty, and to steady themselves, Cariocas speak in a decisive, indubitable way – to name is to call into being. They have an imperial past that can be noticed in their streets, which are named after many dukes and marquis: Marqui of Ouro Preto Street, Baron of Maua Street, Queen Elizabeth Street.

Memorial plaques for dead soldiers line the side wall of the Santa Cruz church, each one has a relief sculpture attached to it: a head with a closed helm and an inscription, "The imperial brotherhood of Santa Cruz from the soldiers to Lieutenant X." Some waiters at bars and hotels serve with an awareness of the dignity of their service. They take care to load up their trays and, when faced with a tricky situation, a mediator always shows up to translate, to illuminate or clarify. Agreement – that's the word – situations must be agreed upon. And harmony does exist, but what prevails is the father's word, the voice of the father, which requires a mediator, some secret meetings to *dar tudo certo* and to pronounce a verdict in that deep, resounding voice. General elections are around the corner and there are no debates playing on Cariocan TV: it seems that undecided voters don't know who the candidates are. But, because it's Father's Day, two center pages of the *Jornal do Brasil* are dedicated to sons paying tribute to their fathers in the following ways:

> My father is better than the rest
> Nobody beats my father
> Father, you are my party.
> My father: the wise and reliable one.
> Join the movement and follow father's lead.
> This election, I vote for my father.

Río bares it all. Referring to Ouvidor Street, a crónica from the turn of the century says: "It's more of a salon than a street." The old and beautiful Ouvidor Street, so well preserved, with its doors and balconies painted blue, and as a backdrop, an orange-colored wall.

Río bares it all: its gardens, its past, its beggars, its beauty, its ugliness. An obese man with two bellies, one on top of the other, is eating at the restaurant. His shirt isn't long enough, but he doesn't mind. Beggars move around the street without fear for themselves or others: one of them was ranting with a very long iron bar in hand – nobody seemed to be frightened. A man with dyed blond hair was dipping a piece of bread inside a can of Coke and offering it to anybody who walked by. Another beggar, a woman this time, was wearing an underskirt that hung behind her like the train of an evening gown. She sat down at a bar next to some middle-class women and drank like any other customer. In the fancy building of the Manchete multimedia complex, a woman was carrying a hamper of clothing from one floor to the next; on top of the hamper, two bras and two pairs of panties were visible – almost tangible – to the people riding the escalator. The past is also revived in this exhibitionism: the property of the Ruy Barbosa foundation, meant for historical and sociological research, has maintained the garden as it's always been, with its enormous palm trees, scaffolding covered in vines, and the same ducks and geese as before. Out front, a sandbox with toys where mothers and their kids are enjoying a snack. It's a museum, a research center, but without the usual stuffiness.

Cariocas do not seem to care for categorical definitions, and they are not eager to point out the difference between how things are and how they should be.

My conversations went more or less like this:

"There should be a crosswalk on this street, it's a dangerous intersection."

Someone in Portuguese:

"There should be one, yes, but there isn't."

And no further remark, because maybe blue elephants should exist, too.

Another conversation in the park:

"Señora, what kind of bird is that?"

"I think it's a rolinha, but I'm not certain."

She consults her mediator: "Do you think it's a rolinha?"

Mediator:

"I think not."

And the conversation ends there – I learned what the bird was not, but there was no need to know more or get to the bottom of things.

On the one hand, Cariocas seem more old-fashioned than Rioplatenses, and on the other, more modern. They seem more old-fashioned because of the words they use – their "agora" and "mesmo" and "mulher" – as if their language were a mixture of Latin and an exotic and fanciful gaucho. But when they leave the beach and walk around the city squeaky clean and half-naked, with only a towel under their arm like a miniscule package, they seem like citizens of the future.

Río bares its dreams and desires through its paintings and crafts. A fresco that embellishes the walls of an Italian restaurant wants to be a Botticelli, but with more intense colors. The door of the restaurant is completely covered by a Nereid wearing a golden crown, a thousand snakes make up the coils in her hair. As two fish nip at her, the siren clutches onto a crab with one hand and a seahorse with the other. Inside the restaurant, an enormous boat takes up all of the floor space that isn't occupied by tables. At a craft fair, I see a pair of crossed arms – they are covered in black velvet and a leather that looks like unborn skin. The hands are not hands, exactly, but talons of some enormous bird of prey. Bejeweled eagle talons. An artist begging for change displays a drawing of a dove with big, green humanlike eyes. The dove wears a furious expression.

Where does the Cariocan fondness for certain names like Eneida, Eneas, Mauritonio, Flavio, and Plinio come from? Perhaps from their imperial past, their taste for biographies and mythologies.

In abundance are educational TV programs that present the myths and history of Rome; the effect is a little postmodern, as if they believed in reincarnation. When Marcus Aurelius tells a centurion: "I'm very busy, I can't help you," the only thing missing from the scene is a cell phone. And they preserve the old way of naming things through epithets, some mythic element that exalts the object, and what's more, calls it into existence. The sign for the Hotel Gloria, alluding to its color, reads, "Our White House." At Posto 6 in Copacabana, a sign in front of a bar reads "A tribute to Frescobol: invented in the 50s, here in Brazil. The only sport with a sportsmanlike spirit, where everyone's a winner." What is Frescobol? Beach paddleball. One renowned comedian is called "the athlete of words," which links together two ideas: a spirit of competition and a battle of wits.

Inside a bridal shop, a maid-of-honor dress catches my eye; it is like an illustration of a fairy dress from a children's book. I say as much to the salesperson, a very pleasant woman.

She replies, "But isn't any wedding a fairy tale?"

She's got a point, but will Brazilians make their own dreams come true? The country has eighteen million (declared) illiterate people. In 1996, Cardoso said that he would enact the necessary reforms to put an end to inequality and turn Brazil into the country of everyone's dreams. But unemployment in Río is still on the rise and it's plain to see this decline in Flamengo, Botafogo, in Copacabana, even, a once semi-elegant neighborhood that's turned into a place where food is sold by the gram. Can the optimism of television, with its well-intentioned educational programs that teach people how to pronounce the word "lawyer," be reconciled with what is seen and experienced? For a long time, Brazilians have considered Cariocas to be lazy, irresponsible, and frivolous. In his impassioned book *Imagery of the Republic of Brazil*, José Murilo de Carvalho recounts how the Republican government was established and how Paulistas distrusted the Cariocas' political decisions. They had their reasons. Three ideologies were used to justify the Republic: liberalism, Jacobinism, and positivism.

Furthermore, Murilo says, "The Republic was established in a moment of economic speculation and a zeal for profit incompatible with Republican virtues."

Not to mention the strong military presence that was equally incompatible with Comte's positivism. On top of that, the Republican party of Río was in crisis; its head Saldanha resigned and wrote to the Paulistas in 1889: "To lead this party is a task well beyond any man's means." A poem of the era, in a desire to harmonize, goes:

> As Brazilians we must
> Against all odds,
> Come together today to show our devotion
> Come forth, monarchists, and you too, anarchists
> Join the positivists with your beating hearts.

During the formation of the Republic, there was no public participation: people did not know what was going on. To add to these challenges, Comte considered the black race to be superior to white and woman superior to man. But, they had to reel it in: finally, after long deliberations about the image of the Republic (if one thing appealed to Comte, it was choosing a mother or some other woman) it was represented by a white woman. The same people who subscribed to Comte's idea that women were superior did not allow women to participate in politics – it went against custom. At the start of the century, the Minister of Finance was accused of reproducing the portrait of his lover on a treasury note, a representation of the Republic.

Concerning this curious inclination to reconcile the irreconcilable, I remember a wigmaker that I met on an earlier trip. She was planning on dancing at Carnival, but she also attended retreats and sermons led by the church to warn the congregation of Carnival's sins and its offenses to God.

"How does that work?" I asked her.

And she replied, "Carnival is lovely, but the priest says lovely things too! It's a pleasure to listen to him."

THE JUNGLES OF LIMA

M ANY YEARS AGO, I visited the city of Iquitos in the Peruvian jungle. To get there you had to – and still have to – fly from Lima. If the river current isn't favorable, it takes around ten days to get there by water. Many humble people were on the plane with me. When we disembarked, they made the sign of the cross. I remember that trip vividly; a multi-colored macaw at the hotel, the hotel's blue walls. The city ascends from the banks of the Marañon, a tributary of the Amazon, and families travel along the river with their kids, dogs, and cooking pots, all inside a canoe. Houses stand on stilts and the rainforest is across from them, at the opposite shore. Near the hotel, a woman protects her homemade breads, which resemble cakes, from the mosquitos. She waves them away with her palm fan, slow and steady. The fan is light-colored like her breads, and the grass and trees of the jungle, a dark green.

Mosquitoes everywhere, even at the tables inside the library. The women who walk along the street are pretty and stand up very straight to carry bundles on their heads. Also on the street, a sign on a house reads: "Doctor will return on May 24th" (it was December). And near the doctor's, the happiest funeral home I've ever seen: a bright-colored mural and a red box decorated with butterflies and flowers hanging above the front door.

A month ago, when I was invited to attend the Lima International Book Fair, I took the opportunity to ask if I could interview an anthropologist, since they are in such abundance there. So they removed me from the travel writing panel and put me on a panel called "Acculturated Ethnic Groups of the Peruvian Amazon." The temptation to participate in that panel went hand in hand with my ignorance: I didn't have any materials in Buenos Aires to find my footing in a meeting like that. I asked them to drop me from the panel as soon as possible and they told me not to worry, that everything would be okay. I don't know if the organizers held shamanic virtues or if they simply said, "No way we're going to move the panelists around again." I ended up on the panel with Cornejo, an anthropologist, and Karina Pacheco, a fiction writer and anthropologist, who gave me two very special books. During the panel, I was "let off the hook," as the kids say.

Then Karina Pacheco said, "Let me introduce you to some interesting people."

Their names were Rebeca and Roger. Rebeca is white and Roger a native man from the Shipibo community in the Amazon rainforest. The two of them, with their son David, form a trinity that goes everywhere together. They go around spreading happiness and promoting Amazonian culture. Roger and Rebeca seem so content as a couple, it's as if they'd only met yesterday. It's an adolescent type of happiness. Their son David is serious, like most teens. He studies Fine Arts in Lima and is the one who photographs and films everything.

Rebeca says excitedly, "He went to New York by himself." And adds: "Stay for the next panel, you'll find it interesting." I stay.

Rember Yahuarcani presents a children's book he illustrated. The author says that he comes from an endangered people, the Witoto, many of whom were displaced because of work or to flee the slavery that rubber barons forced upon them during the Amazon rubber boom. Some Amazonian communities were wiped out completely, others were left with very few people. The presentation is sponsored by the Cultural Center of Spain and there are 5,000 copies of the edition. The book is called *Buinaima's Dream*. It begins with a woman swaying in a serpentine dance, but because she's a Limeña serpent, the dance is discreet. The first panelist is a white woman with the face of a sated cat. She sings Rember's praises. The other panelist, a man from the Andes, is well-prepared for the task. He says, among other things: "Our country owes a huge debt to the Nations of the Amazon, it has abused them, murdered them."

The Andean panelist is dark-skinned, but his skin has more of a matte quality than Rember's. Rember's skin has a shine to it, it's taut and gleaming, and he wears his hair in a bun.

He says, "On my mother's side, I belong to the mother heron clan, and on my father's side, the jaguar clan." He is one of Peru's most important indigenous painters. (Later I found his paintings online, on his website – he really is extraordinary.)

Rember continues, "I would like to honor my grandmother Marta, who passed down the myths to me. Myths serve as answers in the Witoto world; six versions exist, all of them true, about how man and woman first appeared in the world. I see friends here who I have known for ten years, since my arrival in Lima. Together my father and I started looking for ways to introduce words into our language – we worked on finding a translation for 'camera.'"

And despite his paintings being sold in Germany and being in high demand, Rember says, "The illustrations of this book are really paintings – I illustrated this book for people who can't afford to buy my paintings, so they are able to have them."

And, being the child of the rainforest he is, he appreciates smells. He says, "When the book came out, the first thing I loved was that it smelled of freshly printed paper."

. . . . . .

The Peruvian rainforest is home to many ethnic groups that are organized into communities. A host of associations promote the organization of labor, political participation, product sales, while others contribute to improving the natives' quality of life. But when it comes to political participation, not everything that glitters is gold. Even if some native people do become mayors today, mestizos and whites are still granted top positions, while natives are relegated to secondary ones. One might assume that, as a native Polynesian man once said to an anthropologist: "We used to call on the gods for everything; now we call on the district chief." But they manage to find a place for myth in present day reality.

For example, to empower themselves against the mestizos and whites who run businesses, they turn to the myth of Iva and Bachín, which has been passed down through oral storytelling. Iva was a strong and powerful man, and Bachín, a human being who would take the shape of a monkey; he was very sly, a strategist who defeated Iva with his guile. They have also preserved the ritual of taking ayahuasca. The Arawak, for example, take it before deciding which state function serves them best at the moment. Today, many natives work as traders, teachers and professors, chauffeurs, and participate in local politics. But they continue to be invisible to the central authorities and are discriminated against in Lima.

Alan García conceived of Amazonia as an uninhabited land: "A land without men for men without land," he said. He also accused the natives of being "dogs in the manger." When Alan García and Fujimori opened the gates for multinational corporations to exploit the land for oil and gas, this led to the deforestation of the Amazon and native peoples picketed in opposition. Alan García said that the Indians were colluding with foreign powers that were against Peru becoming an oil power. The truth was, the highway strikes were a protest against the contamination of the earth, the water, the air.

WAYS OF PERCEIVING

How do the ethnic groups of the Amazon see the world? Some are descendants of the Arawak, like the guajiros of Colombia, Venezuela, even Cuba, and down through the Peruvian-Ecuadorian-Brazilian rainforest to the Chané of northern Argentina. The Brazilian anthropologist Eduardo Viveiros de Castro says in *The Gaze of the Jaguar*, "They conceive of the world as populated by subjects whose perception of reality differs from the human." For example, the Arameté ethnic group believe that their gods viewed turtles as they did humans. Karina Pacheco, an anthropologist and writer of jungle-themed stories, writes in Gazes, "We weren't collecting the eggs so that we could eat them. My grandfather used to tell us that turtles carry the weight of the world on their backs; if they were to disappear, this weight would befall us and our shells are not designed to support it." And later on, in the same story, "When I touched the skin on my back I could feel a tortoise shell and the indentations of each of its octahedrons and lianas adorning it."

It seems that the Arameté and turtles share a material in common: armor. The turtle's shell appears to be stronger and more resilient than my own spinal column. Daily evidence that my spine is not so strong: when I lean over, or bend down, or do nothing, and still find my back aches. It must be that the turtle's shell and my spine become one entity through their shared status as armor, while jaguars and human beings share a potential for ferocity, or jaguarity.

Unlike the way of thinking in the West, where it is held that human beings and animals have a common past, but that man ultimately triumphed over his animalness, so to speak, here humanity tends to be attributed to animals, to the wind, to inanimate objects even. Karina Pacheco writes: "The sun began to sing in the voice of a cicada," and later: "It began singing in its jaguar voice." According to the Brazilian anthropologist, it is not perspective that makes this cosmovision different from our own, but the world itself. It turns out that forms are at the mercy of forces, and forces change form to manifest themselves as they wish. The rain, the sun, even rocks speak to me. If everything speaks, if everything has something to tell me, the first step to making a decision and to being sure of how I feel is to take a look around – a heron's squawk might give me the answer. It seems strange, but it isn't really. In the past, when I was confused about something, or felt a sense of disquiet, all I had to do was observe my cat's behavior to understand what was going on in me.

The Three Halves of Ino Moxo: Teachings of the Wizard of the Upper Amazon by César Calvo, a writer and journalist from Iquitos, contains many astonishing things. It's a novel composed of short chapters, recounting ayahuasca experiences involving sorcerers and their understudies. The book reminds me of Augusto Roa Bastos's stories. Calvo writes of boa constrictors with ears, fish whose singing used to be audible to us, but whose songs we can no longer register, dogs who become offended when they are offered bananas (because it's human food), flying Christ figures, and butterflies with "velvety" wings. He also mentions police officers who take ayahuasca with their prisoners; "It's fiction," one might say, but even if it is fiction, it's no less astonishing.

In another section of *The Three Halves of Ino Moxo*, a native man arrives early for his flight. He decides to say goodbye to the jungle, since he has time to kill, so he goes near it at first, but ends up getting lost inside and misses his plane. There's a restaurant called "Pucallpa's Baguette" (Pucallpa is a city in the rainforest), because the novel also speaks of everyday things. For example, in today's commercial transactions, distributors (whites and mestizos, for the most part) sell farming and domestic tools to natives. Even though native people pay for these tools, they also believe that the master of the tools is the one who sends them. Since everything – from the mountain and river, to the deity – has a master, the one who allows us to access them is the master. They say that illnesses are not cured with medicinal herbs, but with happiness. Herbs are not valued for their intrinsic qualities but for the manner in which they are given, or prescribed, and the disposition of the person who receives them. Going from one context to another, a doctor who is not careful might give me a remedy that cures me in one way, but makes me ill in another, and if I receive it warily it is very probable that it won't sit well with me.

I also read that it is better to record ideas in the air than in notebooks.

As we know, Fitzgerald, the rubber baron, killed many indigenous people. Ino Moxo, the shaman of Iquitos, said: "When I think about Fitzgerald and his mercenaries, when I think of those genocides, I get the urge to become a citizen of the snakes."

FOR THE CHILDREN OF THE FOREST

Rebeca Rivanadeira, the Limeña teacher who married Roger (the Shipibo leader of Ucajali, Amazonia) wrote *For the Children of the Forest*, a book that tells the story of her life in the rainforest educating local teachers. The book is dedicated to "Roger, my dear husband, to David, the son I always hoped for, and to everyone who is called to serve among the children of the forest."

The part about serving others is connected to Rebeca and Roger being ministers of their evangelical sect. In the book, Rebeca says that her desire to go to the jungle was born when her father, a Limeño journalist, showed her the shrunken Jivaroan heads he kept at home. Rebeca told herself: "I'm going to go there, to the jungle, to find out why they do that." When she was still a young girl she followed through on her promise and caught a first glimpse of the jungle, without telling anyone at home. When she returned, no one believed where she'd gone, so she showed them a souvenir: a pineapple eighty centimeters long and sixty wide. Later she decided to move to Pucallpa, home to three hundred bilingual Catholic and Evangelist teachers and even healers. There she met Roger, who asked her out to a restaurant in Pucallpa. Roger acted like a gentleman, he pulled the chair out for her and passed the sugar bowl so she could serve herself first. She wondered where he'd learned these customs. It turns out that he learned them at the institute for biblical studies.

The natives gave Rebeca the name "Soklo." Since she was on the heavy side and used to wear a blue skirt, they said she looked like that fluffy little blue-winged bird. Later Roger proposed to her and she accepted. She wore a white burlap skirt during the ceremony, with seeds at the hem that rustled when she walked, and a colorful crown on her head. Roger wore a crown with three feathers.

And finally, after three miscarriages, David, the son that accompanies them everywhere, was born.

A VISIT TO THE CANTAGALLO COMMUNITY

It seems that what connects Rebeca to the people of the Peruvian jungle is the belief that almost anything is possible. She had three miscarriages while she was with Roger and told him that she would not have any more children, and then David was born. She went against the wishes of her relatives in Lima and married a Shipibo man; she fell off a boat into the Amazon and everyone thought she had drowned, and still she never abandoned what she calls her mission.

Rebeca was my guide to the Shipibo community in Cantagallo, which is close to the Rimac River in Lima's old town. Cantagallo is what we would call a shantytown in Buenos Aires, while Peruvians use the euphemism "young town." There are no sewers in Cantagallo, so people retrieve water from a well; the streets are slightly uneven, all unpaved. The houses are made from flimsy materials and painted in all colors, especially blue, red, and yellow. Cantagallo has a bilingual school, but it's closed because of a public holiday. Four boys, from about six to eleven, are playing nearby.

I ask, "Who here was born in Lima?"

The three smallest ones raise their hands and the eldest says he was born in the rainforest. He remembers little from back then, but he's gone back to visit once.

Rebeca, Roger, and David came out to greet me all at once, like a little traveling troupe that goes everywhere. David has a heavy-duty camera. They had already spoken with Roldán and Roxana, who were expecting me at Roxana's house. I talk to Jonás beforehand. He's the founder of the community and the bilingual school. Born in the rainforest, he's been in Lima for the past fifteen years.

He says, "The food of the rainforest is healthier than Lima's. Everything is cooked over the fire and they don't use spices, and everyone keeps their doors open because break-ins are rare. When people beg, they receive what they need."

He tells me about how rainforest customs are more hygienic. In Cantagallo, kids have a lot of skin problems because of the lack of sewers; in the rainforest, after doing their business, people wipe with a banana leaf. I ask him about the other differences he sees in Lima and he says that love is different, that in the Amazon, it is still custom for the father of the bride to give his daughter away, and she is expected to obey his wishes.

We go inside Karina's house to meet her and Roldán, a painter. It's easy to forget that the house is a precarious construction because you are confronted with color at every corner, from the walls – where Roldán's paintings are hanging – to his work table, where he makes his handicrafts, necklaces, bracelets, wind chimes, miniature canoes, and paddles. His canoes are opaque, a natural red, and his drawings are black. It's a wooden red, in complete harmony with the figure of the canoe; you can imagine the plant from which the dye was extracted. His wind chimes are made of fish teeth, and I see a necklace made from blue seeds that would be considered a treasure anywhere.

Roldán's paintings include jaguars, boas, herons, monkeys, and turtles. He sells his paintings in Germany; he's traveled to Germany and Japan, but continues to live in the Cantagallo community. He hands me his business card. One side features a creature, its body covered in nervures, as if it were both vegetable and animal. Two names appear on the back of the card. At the top: Shoyan Sheca. And at the bottom: Shipibo-Konibo Artist. In the center, in bigger letters: Roldán Pinedo López. And an address: Vía Evitamiento 6, Third Floor, Cantagallo market, Rimac, Lima, Peru. He tells me that Shoyan Sheca was the name given to him by the community, it means "restless mouse."

He says, "My grandfather was a shamanic healer. In the rainforest, stories and myths are passed down to children. Some animals foretell a long life, like the turtle, while owls announce the arrival of a visitor. One bird, the *sharara*, catches fish while flying. Then the man says: 'How I'd love to be a bird, so I could catch fish while flying.' My first exhibition in Lima was in 1999 and memories of the jungle come to me here, so I paint them and it brings me happiness."

Karina is pretty and reticent, around thirty or so; she works while he talks. I'm told that she has recently suffered a tragedy: her husband passed away before his fortieth birthday. But I suspect that she is experiencing the fluctuations of the transition: she belongs neither here nor there. She has her traditional costume on, but it is prudent, disguised.

She says, in passing, "My grandmother used to predict the future. She's in Lima now. Her interpretations came from dreams and from watching animals. My great-grandfather had two wives, which was legal back then; sisters would often be taken as wives, it was legal."

Roger says, "I am grateful to Karina's grandfather. He saved my life. My mom buried me when I was born, and he rescued me." – This was common practice when there were too many kids, and other circumstances, and he says it without emphasis, like when you give thanks for a present – "I changed my name many times: Juan, Tomás, García, but it couldn't be Juan because I already had a brother with that name. At eighteen, I found out that García was a last name. My older brother named all of us and our birth dates were decided by the civil registry. My sister told me that I was not born on the date they had written, that I was born during watermelon season. Here in Lima, I learned to look people in the eye, because in the jungle it's different, you look above or below, never straight on."

Here Rebeca jumps in, "I used to say to Roger, 'Tell me that you love me.'"

"Things are different there," Roger says. "How is affection shown?

The wife prepares a meal that her husband likes, or the husband stays with his wife instead of going fishing."

I ask Roger to tell me about the most common insults. For someone slow, you could call them a "lazy *panshe*," or "sloth," like the animal. Another insult is "skinny monkey." He says: "When a boy doesn't have a father, it's shameful; he is born, but cannot grow."

Returning to his many names and to his life in the jungle, he says, "I've lived a life of dichotomy, and people in the jungle live like that too, when they're sick they go to see the pastor, the priest, the shaman, the spiritual guide, who all tell them different things."

Both Roger and Roldán are wearing traditional jackets with geometric drawings. Roger's has a sign.

Rebeca says, "You put 'Nibake'" – son of the jungle – "on your jacket."

And they both turn around so I can see the other side of the coat.

"Show her your waistband, Karina."

Karina lifts her red blouse to reveal a broad white waistband, a sign of her status: she is the descendant of a shaman. Later she tells me that there are thousands of people from distinct indigenous groups in Lima and the association that she chairs shares Amazonian art with Limeños. Her eldest daughter, a nineteen-year-old, studies environmental administration in the city.

. . . . . .

Many things astonished me during this visit, and during my trip as a whole. First, that Limeños are unaware of the existence of jungle communities in the city; second, that the talents of their painters and artisans is undeniable. Also, the history of these peoples, who rejected the conquistadors, the Incas, and the Sendero Luminoso guerrilla fighters who went to look for followers but did not find them. In one of his stories, Daniel Alarcón suggests that the greatest difficulty the guerrilla fighters faced in the jungle was not combat, which was rare, but the heat, insects, and the stretches of time spent waiting, listening to unknown sounds – these were the real enemies.

I would go to the jungle if only to do that, to listen to new, unknown sounds.

NOT MEANT TO BE

WHEN I WAS IN PERGAMINO, Señor X said, "Tapalqué is ideal for what you're looking for, the town creates its own refrains. People are constantly repeating and altering them; take my word for it and go see Capdevila. I suggest you buy his book, he's collected a ton of refrains and you'll see just how many originated from that area."

Señor X had a point, and while skimming that book of refrains in a Pergamino cafe, I said to myself, "One day, I will go to Tapalqué."

It was a kind of path, a duty, and a source of potential happiness, two years in the making. I'd forget about Tapalqué and then be reminded of it, as if it had always been there waiting for me. Sometimes, when I was a little depressed, it would occur to me that Capdevila was probably dead (Señor X had mentioned his old age), but in my more upbeat moments, I figured that even if he weren't still alive, he would have left behind a school, something. About a month ago, I couldn't decide where to go and suddenly I remembered Tapalqué, so one weekend in mid-January while everyone was on holiday, I set off for that town without any contacts, guided by some higher power.

When I got off the bus, I asked the young woman behind the counter, "Could you please recommend a clean and affordable hotel with a private bathroom?"

A man was by her side, chatting quietly with her. I was the only passenger who had gotten off at Tapalqué.

The man said, "We don't have any hotels here; we used to have one, but the mayor couldn't decide what to do with it, it's been under construction for the past four years. You should bring it up with the mayor."

I glanced at the bus station: it was no bigger than my living room, without a newspaper or cigarette kiosk, or even a café, so I said, "No cafés at this terminal?"

"You ask for a lot," the man said, and the young woman at the ticket counter said kindly, "You can stay at Mary's house, she's a good person."

The man said, "Mary went to Buenos Aires for the weekend."

"Then you could go to Lola's instead," the young woman said courteously.

Perking up, I added, "I was told that this town creates its own criollo refrains, some of the wittiest around."

The man said, "The person who told you that must've had one too many. Take my advice, visit the museum tomorrow. My wife will be there – tell her I sent you. She knows everything."

I asked, "And what's your name, sir?"

"Beto." He looked at me in amazement for not knowing his name. I must be the only person in the world who doesn't know Beto.

The woman at the counter called a cab driver and said, "Take her to Lola's."

The driver asked me to speak up because he had trouble hearing out of his left ear; I launched straight into the topic of refrains and he said that yes, many people use refrains, but unfortunately, he didn't have the phone number of any refrain-makers, coupleteers, or bards. He drops me off at Lola's house, a little white house that's clean as can be, and Lola is waiting for me by the door.

I explain what I'm doing in Tapalqué and she says, "Business?"

"Not business," I say, as foreigners do in those conversations where both people turn into Tarzan, and say things like: "Not tea, coffee" or "Not near, far." I ask her if she knows of anyone who might practice the art of the refrain.

She says, "What's a refrain?"

"Well," I say, "For example, 'In the blacksmith's house, all knives are wooden.'"

Right then it became clear that Señora Lola hadn't heard of this refrain, that I had chosen wrong, that refrains were worth shit, and that I didn't have the faintest idea of what I was doing in that house.

She says, "Me, I don't know anything about such things. I'm a woman of the house. I leave my house to go to work and leave work to come home."

Troubled, but still wanting to say something, I ask, "And where do you work, Señora?"

"At home," she said, smiling.

At this stage, I no longer wanted her to work at all, for anybody, so I grabbed my bag and said, "I'm sorry for bothering you, Señora. I should go."

I gave her twenty pesos for her time, but she didn't seem bothered by my departure – she didn't care either way. So, I took my tune elsewhere, to another town.

REFRAINS AND SAYINGS

Enthusiastic by my visit to the outskirts of Pergamino, I bought a book that contained criollo sayings and refrains, compiled by Capdevila. He points out that the inhabitants of Tapalqué in the Buenos Aires province have been creating local sayings and refrains for a long time, repeating them and coming up with new ones to this day. For example, some women from Méndez used to say, "Since our guest cannot stay, let us hit the hay" when they were ready for their visitor to leave. One man, when asked how he was getting along, replied, "Like a poor man's ass." In Tapalqué, they say of a very cluttered house, "It's got more frills than Burgos's bed."

Aside from Tapalqué, two refrains in the collection appear in the writings of Fray Mocho, the great costumbrista of the 1880s. To describe an indecisive person, the refrain goes: "Round and round like a dog lying down." For someone who's got a lot of excuses, needs, and demands, you use the refrain: "He's got a lot of fine print." Referring to the fine print that appears at the end of contracts, the saying shows how the city permeates the country and vice versa. This fluid interplay between city and country can be found in Fray Mocho's writings. A typical character of his is the rancher who, after becoming rich, moves to the nearest city – to Buenos Aires, if he has the chance – without losing his criollo speech, mannerisms, and metaphors, which tend to be clever and accurate.

One character who appears in a crónica of Fray Mocho's, a mother, complains to her friend and companion that all of her daughters married foreigners after coming to Buenos Aires. She says, "If I had known this would happen, I would've sent them off for a few laps around Pergamino and called it a day." Each daughter married a foreigner of distinct origins, and the mother says of the Frenchman, "That Frenchie, he shakes hands like a chained sparrow." And the observation is precise because, even today, the French do not extend their elbows while shaking hands.

Back to the subject of refrains, criollo wisdom tends to be linked to some quality or flaw in animals, which are considered archetypes, although criollo is often in awe of the characteristics of a particular animal as well. So this connection with animals turns out to be ambivalent. On the one hand, there is a stark difference between animal and person; on the other hand, most refrains point to the intimate relationship between human and animal behavior. The very myth of the werewolf points to the possibility of changing from one to the other. A woman in Mercedes told me that, in her youth, she and her girlfriends used to chat about the birth order of potential suitors: under no condition should they be seventh-born sons. The girls didn't aspire to marry someone handsome, rich, or intelligent – the important thing was that he didn't turn into a werewolf. A rural man from Mercedes told me that armadillos cross their front feet and cry out movingly when they're being slaughtered. The man added, "In their cries they say: *Jesus, Jesus!*"

Animals are examples of many different behaviors and attitudes. In small towns, people tend to greet each other, but some greet more often than others. The refrain goes: "Friendly as a lapwing." For suspicious people: "more suspicious than a one-eyed horse" or "belligerent as a one-eyed rooster," since his poor eyesight makes the rooster think everyone's out to get him. Acting like a foal means playing dumb, and when it comes to someone who doesn't know what they're talking about: "What's a donkey know 'bout cakes if he's never been a baker?" When a situation is routine, monotonous, the refrain is "always the same ole sheep face." And it's true, sheep do look a lot like one another. The book includes universal refrains that have a criollo spin. A Spanish refrain: "The good always comes with the bad," and its criollo addition: ". . . a crippled old lady told me"; or this one: "It depends on your tastes, said an old woman — and she swallowed an espadrille." The revised refrains indicate, without saying so directly because the criollo style is elusive, that some things are objectively worse than others, and same goes for ugliness. Another refrain on the subject: "It's ugly. . . an armadillo covered in sugar."

Other refrains refer to people's intelligence or reliability. When someone not typically prone to insight or subtlety says something interesting, they say: "My dog caught a fly." When someone is unreliable, promises and doesn't deliver, or says irrelevant things: "Pure foam, like the screamer." Intrigued by the foam produced by the southern screamer, I searched for explanations among country folk (some of them veterinarians), and they gave me distinct answers: one, when the screamer is irritated it secretes a lot of foam, making it toxic to predators. But I'm more convinced by another interpretation: apparently, the screamer has very little edible meat on its bones.

Lapwings and ostriches seem to have inspired a special curiosity, given how many refrains refer to them: "He crouches like a lapwing marking his territory." It's also the prototype for secretive people: "The lapwing screeches in one place and lays eggs in another" (to protect its nest). Referring to the outcome of a game: "They plucked him like an ostrich." And, to illustrate an unusual situation: "Where was the ostrich seen gargling?" There's a refrain for everything. For formality: "Formal as a donkey in the corral." For solitude: "Going around like an orphaned egg" and this delightful one: "Everyone's got their little someone, I've got my little old me." There are other sayings that refer to objects and situations: new soap, before it is used, is called "virgin soap." To describe someone who skips important steps in a process: "He hasn't learned to trot, but wants to gallop." When a horse bucks a rider and leaves him belly up, looking at the sky, the saying goes: "He's left looking at the constellations."

While criollos use sarcasm to allude to human vices and virtues in its animal metaphors, it tends to be diplomatic and doesn't escalate conflict. Instead of calling someone who crosses the line "nosy," "meddlesome," or "invasive," they say: "Don't go to the patio or you'll step on the chickens." They are not ones for direct reproaches or quick value judgments. Instead of saying to your opponent, "You're wrong," a softer alternative might be, "It seems to me, Roldán, that not all of these cows are yours."

Here's a beautiful one: "Soft as a little angel's heel."

Finally, two wise refrains: "Nobody dies from an almost." And this one: "You must first get lost before leading the way."

OFF TO MEXICO

IN 2014, ARGENTINA WAS the guest of honor at the Guadalajara International Book Fair, the largest book fair in Latin America. The Chancellery, Ministry of Culture, and provincial governments sent sixty or so fiction writers and ten TV journalists to discuss social and political subjects related to Argentina. Around ninety editors were also invited to sell their books, along with a number of journalists from the capital and interior to report on the fair and organize panels and other events. The ambassador gathered around three hundred people at the Chancellery and vehemently told them, "Remember to attend each other's panels and events." (Don't even think about going to see the mariachis or a replica of the Feathered Serpent while your colleagues are left with empty seats for the "Are writers born or made?" debate.) She added, "And the lanyard goes around your neck." (Meaning there is always some black sheep who forgets their lanyard, is banned from entering, and becomes her problem.)

All of this worried me. Seeing as I wanted to write a crónica on Guadalajara, I would need free time to wander the streets and decipher the thousands of things I'd read about and didn't understand, for example "ni madres," which is another way of saying, "no way." "Ese viejo se las truena" (he's high) or "vete a la chingada," sending someone off to a distant, indeterminate place.

I was overwhelmed by it all: the hundreds of words I didn't understand, the size of the book fair, and the lanyard I had to wear to avoid getting kicked out. Lately I've been overwhelmed by big places because everything is so spread out.

On the plane, my seat mate was a Mexican man in a khaki suit, with jet-black eyes.

"Were you in Buenos Aires for pleasure?"

"No, I went on a mission trip to Tucumán, Salta, and Jujuy. I'm a Mormon."

"And do the ones from Salta and Jujuy go on mission trips to Mexico?"

"Exactly," he said.

At first, I didn't understand the reasons behind these trips, but later I realized it was training for young missionaries, a way for them to learn the tools of the trade, so to speak. The young man had learned to express himself in parables. Once, he had felt a strong presence;

it was the prophet speaking to him, telling him to lay on his hands, just as Jesus had done. From what I could understand, the missionary's journey was a metaphor for life. We are born blind, without knowledge, like the missionary setting forth on his journey. By the time we complete the mission, we are older, more seasoned.

"Ah!" I said.

"For now, I'm going back to my normal life in Veracruz."

Normal life meant marrying his girlfriend and studying architecture and sculpture because he wanted to be a sculptor. It's not that the last two years had been abnormal, but that people experience one lifecycle inside another. I gave up listening to him once he started repeating how he'd manifested the prophet, but when the food arrived, I saw that he was very agile with his hands. He took the plastic off the container in one fell swoop, same with his pre-packaged blanket, and in no time at all he was eating, with relish, a paste with disguised bits of floating chicken. And it wasn't odd. Because what did Jonas eat in the stomach of the whale? Half-digested fish.

. . . . . .

Guadalajara spreads out in every direction; it takes me almost ten minutes to get from my room to the reception desk. The hotel is rated five stars, but everything is low to the ground. There are no elevators, only stairs that lead to a second floor, and despite being a top-tier hotel, the room is peculiar. To start, it has an ironing board, but no bidet, and in the place of a shower screen, there's a curtain with a logo on it. The furniture is enormous and square, a kind of writing table that four people could eat lunch on, and very hard upright chairs.

"Could I ask for your autograph?" a maid says.

And I ask for a caramel in return. It's dulce de leche.

In the hotel lobby, I spot what appears to be a Christmas tree with a birdcage hanging on it (and birds inside), some kind of pot with coffee beans, and a gnome dressed head to toe in winter clothes riding a wooden bicycle. Another gnome, wearing a colorful cooking apron, holds on to a cage. Some plants are balanced on flimsy wooden fruit crates. I don't understand the meaning of this arrangement, and I remember what Octavio Paz said about Mexicanness: "A taste for decorations, carelessness, and pomp." And Carlos Monsiváis, the great essayist, adds something similar: "Love for the unnatural, the artificial, the exaggerated – an appreciation of vulgarity." This appreciation of vulgarity can be seen in the old fruit crates that are used as plant stands, and exaggeration, in the enormous manger in a crowded street. Baby Jesus will soon be visited by a colossal elephant.

Another Mexican characteristic Octavio Paz points to is dissimulation. The ideal, stand-up guy does not back down, reveal himself, or betray his true feelings. He who shows emotion is a coward. Paz says that, from childhood, men are taught to be patient and stoic.

There is a popular song about this subject:

Impassioned heart,
Disguise your sorrow,
Disguise your sorrow,
Impassioned heart.

Guadalajarans are courteous. I tell the maid that I'll be going to bed early, but that I plan on watching a bit of TV first.

"The TV will lull you to sleep," she says. And when she notices that I've made a wrong turn on my way to the reception, she says, "Just go straight and turn at that big old tree. Or we could go together."

. . . . . .

We were assigned guides, or guardian angels, to take us from the book fair to the hotel and wherever else we needed to go. I had Alejandra, Yolanda, and Clara. Our chauffeur, Hector, knew a lot about Mexican history and politics.

"I'd like to see a local home," I say.

"Let's go to my granny's then," says Alejandra.

"It won't bother her, us barging in?"

"No way."

We head to a neighborhood near an orphanage, and Hector says, "My mother-in-law grew up there."

We go inside Alejandra's grandmother's house and there she is, Grandma Luz, with her legs stretched out in front of her. She is unable to walk. I think she must be furious, but in the Mexican way, that is, a disguised fury. She used to be beautiful and Hector says that Tapatías, or women from Jalisco, are the most beautiful women in all of Mexico. I try my best to make conversation with Luz, but nothing sticks.

"What a cozy house," I say.

"It's very poorly built, too square in the front. A nuisance."

Ever the optimist, I continue, "Do you have any pets?"

"No, never liked them."

So I take the route of childhood memories.

"My father was mugged and killed."

"What about your mother?"

"Left when I was two years old."

She said all of this frankly, with measured statements. Only once did she smile, just a little, when we talked about food. She said she liked caldo de pollo, a chicken soup often served at restaurants. Before I can determine if she's annoyed or disinterested, it's time for us to leave. Along the way, Alejandra tells me that her grandfather, Luz's husband, left Luz alone with five kids, including Alejandra's mother. Luz went to the United States to find work and left the kids with an acquaintance. Grandma Luz told Alejandra that she considered jumping off the train on the way there and ending it all, but the thought of her five children waiting for her back in Mexico gave her the will to keep going.

Not long after we left, I fell. We were heading to Tlaquepaque with Alejandra and Yoli to look at folk art and listen to mariachi music, and I fell facedown, catching myself on my wrists, knees, and nose, which bled a little, leaving me with a bloody mustache and some other bloody spots on my forehead and below the eye. I was left with a slight limp. On the way down, I thought that the fall would be intense, but not fatal – an "almost" fall. The blood I lost, though not very much, made things look blurry. My guardian angels took me to the University hospital, which receives an astounding number of patients. A doctor asked the nurse to give me an injection for the pain. She was one of those fun-loving women with plump cheeks, always smiling. We were in a little room with a man sitting up in a stretcher.

I said to her, "I've never gotten an injection in front of a man."

"Don't worry," she said, "He's practically blind." Then, to him: "Turn around."

The man turned around, indifferent; she gave me the injection and we left. Some people were sitting on the curb of a nearby street, eating soups and stews. The hospital gives them out.

THE FAIR

The Guadalajara Book Fair is the largest in Latin America, and so is the traffic jam to get there. We arrived at the front entrance early, all of us in our official lanyards, but since we couldn't find parking, we circled around for a kilometer or two. The driver doesn't complain.

I ask the driver, "What if we had come by foot?"

"It's about 5 kilometers, no way."

We had just arrived when I started thinking about how nice it would be to go to the hotel to watch television (they have every channel in the world). I'd had my share of book fairs, but new channels . . . We arrived fairly quickly to the exhibition hall, which had an enormous table with the names of the presenters: two Mexicans, Argentina, that was me, and Mario Delgado Aparaín from Uruguay. I'd known that I was going to be on the panel with Mario – I was looking forward to seeing him again. We hadn't seen each other since a conference in Berlin some twenty years ago. It was back when no one cared about chasing down smokers; still, the Germans sent us down to some basement filled with succubi so that we could all smoke and suffer together. Everything in its rightful place. I wanted to see him because he had written a beautiful book, *Don't Steal the Boots of the Dead*, about the Siege of Paysandú, in Uruguay, where he details the events leading up to the Paraguay War.

Every writer was asked to define their writerly creed and I was a bit alarmed because I hadn't prepared any kind of creed, but then I remembered that everyone says what comes to mind at these panels, whatever they want (at times I've even seen people argue with the moderator or audience members), so I calmed down. The writer who was sitting beside me had a Mayan look to him, an oval-shaped face.

He said, "I believe in the syntax of teachers who have moved me; I believe in nameless texts, revelations left unsaid."

While he spoke, I tried to remember what I believed, but nothing came to me. Later, another Mexican writer defined literature as a spacious mansion, the novel as a big house with a garden, where you can get some fresh air. The essay was the foundation of the house, and poetry, a corner – sister of the short story.

And Mario wasn't there for any of this. Had he gotten lost at the fair?

Another author read a short story about a global cataclysm. It seems as though the men became more modest – less vain – as the cataclysm neared. I was saddened by what the author had chosen to destroy: Colombia, which was left unrecognizable. Poor, lovely Colombia, I thought. Then the men wandered around in circles (the world had changed, where there were once toothbrushes, now lay moon rocks). "They were quantum nomads," the author said. And who had he decided to save? Philosophers, don't ask why. At long last, Mario Delgado arrived and I cheered up. Turns out, he really had gotten lost at the fair. Well aware of the fact that he was speaking to a Mexican audience who wasn't acquainted with the Paraguay War, he spoke quite plainly of the Siege of Paysandú, of the war, and he captivated everyone.

. . . . . .

The next day my guardian angels, Alejandra and Yolanda, and I went to the Hospicio Cabañas, a building reminiscent of both a church and prison. It dates back to 1810, when it was opened as a refuge for poor elderly women and abandoned children. We go to see Orozco's frescoes, which are along the inner walls of the courtyards. Our guide walks with a cane and says that the building, with its twenty courtyards, is the biggest of its kind in America. It's been declared a world heritage site.

The main courtyard is dry and austere, not a plant in sight. A group of twenty or so kids are touring the museum with their teachers; they're between seven and eleven years old. A teacher calls one of her girls "mamacita" and another "reina." The guide tells the kids to settle down, and not only that, he also lectures them on the rules they'll need to follow if they want to stay on the tour. One rule is that you're not allowed to stick chewing gum anywhere because the bacteria might harm the artwork. Later he asks them to repeat the name of the Hospicio's founder, "the illustrious Doctor Señor Juan Cabañas y Crespo." Since they are, of course, unable to repeat after him, it becomes a form of comedic discipline, and after the guide shares so much of the illustrious lineage, they repeat after him: "Uno, dos, tres, mambo!"

He shows them the fresco of Hernán Cortés on the ceiling and tells them that Orozco painted Cortés like a robot because of the things he wore, armor and other peculiar things. The kids settle down.

Back at the hotel, I overhear someone say "chin." They say it's used as an interjection when someone messes up, or falls, and is equivalent to "damn it" or "oh, shit." I also learned "macuarro" (poor quality), "no hagas coraje" (chill out), and "madrear," which means to beat up.

. . . . . .

We head to the town of Ajijic, sixty or so kilometers outside of Guadalajara, together with Héctor who says "sí" in a patient and faintly singsong voice, as if he were speaking with kids. Then there's Yolanda, who carries an enormous tote bag filled with what most people would pack for a three- or four-day trip (she's got sleeping pills that give her heartburn and other pills to treat the heartburn). Zulema and Clara are with us too; Zulema is quiet as can be and Clara, a firecracker.

"Tapatíos never say what's on their mind, but not me, when I'm riled up everybody knows it. People are so fucking annoying!"

Walking around the book fair, we stopped a young man to ask him something. Supposedly, he should have known the answer, but he was a little slow.

Clara said to him, "Oh, honey, come on. Do you know anything at all?" Turning to me: "Kid's a dunce."

Ajijic looks like a toy town, full of colorful little houses embellished with flowers, bees, and tchotchkes. In the plaza, I see lots of red flowers, fire-flowers.

One house has stained glass windows, a dome; another hotel is called "Humphrey Bogart." Many of the signs are in English, but despite the Aztec monolith in the plaza, half of the town's residents are gringos. Retired Americans and Canadians are the people who live comfortably around here. They don't fraternize with the local population and can be seen basking in the sun in café patios around the plaza, speaking in English and pampering their dogs. Also spotted, hippies and foreign neohippies. Local Mexican kids that go from table to table selling trinkets, or begging for change; the gringos' wealth does not spill over.

A man sitting on a bench in the plaza, a Mexican by the looks of it, says to me, "Yes, this town is propped up by retired gringos, we've got Canadians and an Argentinian woman who sells nieve. There's ten thousand of us here, five thousand are gringos who live here year-round and in winter we're joined by ten thousand more. We locals call them "winter birds" because they fly south for the winter."

His bench-mate is an old man with snow-white whiskers; when I begin to chat with his friend and ask him questions, he gets silent, retreats into his inner chambers. I can't tell if he doesn't like that

I'm talking to his companion or if it's just not his turn to speak. Or maybe one should only speak when spoken to directly. In the middle of the plaza there's a pavilion with a red roof trimmed in gold – it reminds me of wire, a large birdcage. A woman walks past with a kid and says to him: "Come on, chiquillo!" A man goes by shouting "pacholas, pacholas" (meat patties), but no customers appear.

We sit down in a little café along the sidewalk and Zulema, the shy young woman, says, "I've got a big sweet tooth."

Héctor remarks that Ajijic, with its ten thousand inhabitants, has a much wider variety of cheese, beer, and sweets in its supermarkets than Guadalajara does with its six million.

Clara, referring to the gringos, says, "Bastards!"

But we instantly forget about these social injustices and begin exchanging Creole sayings from our corners of the world. They tell me one that goes:

> If you don't like to straddle
> and your horse makes you itch,
> drop your steed and your saddle,
> you damn son of a bitch.

This is my last outing in Guadalajara. Tomorrow I will be in gigantic Mexico City, alone, without my governesses, limping from the fall.

In Guadalajara, the book fair and outings with my guides gave me a solid foundation for the crónica. But Mexico City overwhelms me with its historical and political past, a past so rich, and so peculiar. So I began rereading books about the conquest and things of that nature. In *The Labyrinth of Solitude*, Octavio Paz writes: "We are now certain of the fact that the great creative era of Mesoamérica precedes the Aztecs' arrival in the Anáhuac valley by several centuries."

Among these peoples, the Mixtec poet-philosophers used to ruminate in beautiful gardens, which existed for the very purpose of stirring the mind.

There's a Nahuatl poem that goes like this:

> I perceive the secret, the hidden
> Oh, señores!
> So we are,
> We are mortal
> Four by four
> We men will depart
> We will all die on Earth
> Like a painting
> We will fade
> Like a flower

We will wither
On this very land
Like the feathers of the Zacuán
That precious lithe-necked bird
We will fall to the ground.

Interesting, too, is the Mayan creation myth recounted in the Popol Vuh. It says that, in the beginning, there was a vast emptiness and silence. The Framer and the Shaper began to put every creature in its place. But since they could not make the animals speak, "only shriek, each with a distinct cry," they set out to create a being who could speak and name everything that existed, and so they created humans. Things turned out poorly for the Framer and Shaper because their humans were able to speak but could not understand each other . . . It's curious, this creation myth, because of its experimental nature: first came those delicate mud beings who could speak but not communicate; later the gods created wooden dolls that multiplied into stick dolls. But they didn't have souls or memory of their creators – they wandered around aimlessly, on all fours. After they were destroyed, the gods created human beings.

A dramatic poem depicts the arrival of the conquistadors (it details the thriving world of before, the absence of diseases, and people who used to walk with their heads held high):

But the conquistadors arrived
and everything came undone.

They taught fear, they withered the flowers,
and drank from the flower of others
to keep their own alive.

They killed the Nacxitl flower.
No longer were there priests among us.
And that's how the second half came,
dominated, and led to our death.

Without priests, or wisdom, or courage
all of them equal, lacking shame.
The conquistadors had only come to castrate the sun!

Let's see how Bernal Díaz del Castillo, chronicler of the conquest,
tells the story:

One morning a courtyard was crowded with Indians and their
wives burning a species of resin, which is similar to our incense.
We stopped to observe the scene closely and an old Indian
man climbed atop a temple. He was the priest of those Indians. Cortés asked Melchorejo, who understood their language

very well, to interpret what the old Indian man was saying. Upon discovering that he was preaching evil things, Cortés ordered the caciques to sacrifice the idols that were leading them astray. The caciques replied that if we rid them of their idols, we would experience the power they possess once we find ourselves lost at sea.

Cortés orders the idols be smashed to pieces and puts an image of the Virgin Mary in their place.

On their march to Mexico City in 1519: "The houses stood on water and one had to travel by means of bridges and canoes to go from one house to another. Every house had a balcony at the top and might be used as a fortress."

When Cortés and Moctezuma met each other: "Moctezuma was beneath a sedan of silver and pearls, with great swaths of gold and green feathers (…) He was wearing golden soles on his feet (…) Several Indians would sweep the ground where Moctezuma stepped and lay rugs before him so that his feet would never touch the ground. (…) They would not look at him in the face."

In another meeting, the Indians came with several artists and painted Cortés, his soldiers, and their greyhounds. Later they presented the final portrait to Moctezuma. (These Aztec codices are in the Museum of Anthropology – which takes three days to see in its entirety – they are made from fig-bark paper, with an infinite number of painted scenes, since history used to be told through pictorial language.)

Back to Moctezuma and Cortés. In the beginning they brought Cortés plenty to eat as well as cloths embroidered with tigers, suns, and stags (they were great illustrators) but it seems that later, Moctezuma's idols told him to stop listening to Cortés, and so the provisions came less often. There was an insider among the caciques and Moctezuma.

Bernal Díaz del Castillo says, "The fat cacique complains to Cortés that Moctezuma orders too many of his children be sacrificed, and takes his wives and daughters by force."

Returning again and again to that characteristic that Monsiváis and Octavio Paz talk so much about: could dissimulation have historic origins? They were forced to conceal their true intentions from Cortés so that he wouldn't rob them of all they had; conceal themselves from Moctezuma, safely hide their children so they wouldn't be taken away; conceal themselves from tribute collectors, who also ripped them off . . . And some depressing news I hear recently: certain mothers, afraid of the narcos kidnapping their daughters for god only knows what, make them look so ugly that they are no longer desirable.

Here in the city, everything is monumental in size. The artisan market, with its endless stalls, is dizzying, the Museum of Anthropology is more or less unmanageable, the Library of Mexico contains about fifteen long courtyards, and Insurgentes Avenue, which extends from the north to the south of the city, is over sixty kilometers long and still falls within city limits. At this moment, the D.F. contains around twenty-nine million inhabitants. I am in the Zócalo, a historic center where the central plaza, National Palace, local government, and cathedral are located. How is it they measure blocks here? My hotel is on Antonio Caso 83 Street, and there are four blocks between 1 and 83. The National Palace, red and made of stone, has about ten thousand little windows. So much stone, and red, because of all the red and silver Christmas decorations. It's been over a month since they've started preparing for Christmas and the central plaza is sealed off. Why? Because they're going to install a skating rink in front of the cathedral. That ancient red stone reminds me of Aztec sacrifice and of the murders of leaders and presidents. Zapata, Pancho Villa, and the Austrian emperor who came to Mexico to put things in order, all died by assassination. According to Octavio Paz, the conquest represents the defeat and the death of Quetzalcoatl, the creator of the world; even the gods died.

But today taxis of every color go by on the streets, some of them with drawings of flowers or animals; some are red, some light blue, green, and white. On the side of a bus (or "truck," as they call it) it says, "We don't follow the rules, we make our own." Another sign on a minibus: "Do you feel the itch of an idea?" A bike taxi goes by, like the ones in Cuba, and right in front of the cathedral, a man plays a creaky ballad on a little organ. Next door, beside the temple, pictures of Pancho Villa, the Beatles, Cantinflas, Frida Kahlo, and Che are on sale. Inside the front courtyard of the cathedral: "Given that this is the Templo Mayor, all vendors are prohibited." All of the vendors are outside, together with those who beg for change. Inside the cathedral, the priest blesses people and objects: rosaries, images. A woman approached the altar holding a balloon. Would it be blessed, too?

I turn a corner and find a pedestrian street filled with people. The crowd is so big that I get the urge to duck away for a while and regain my strength before facing the street again. I sit down at a cafe called "Vamos al grano" and order something to eat. I watch people pass by; they smile at each other despite being strangers. The ground is a kaleidoscope – not one mosaic is the same as the other. One tile has white flowers with a green background, another beside it has red flowers on yellow, an array of geometric designs on blue, and so on. Could it be that this tile design is faithful to some ancient Aztec decor, just as the Virgin of Guadalupe, the patroness of Mexico, seems to be a continuation of Tonantzin, the goddess of fertility? Uniformity does not exist, not in the color of taxis, the floor tiles of the cafe, or the objects blessed in the cathedral. I can't quite get a sense of the Mexican way, my banged up leg hurts, and I take a cab to the hotel, which is tucked away in a corner, a refuge of sorts.

THE CUSTOM OF KILLING

Octavio Paz, referring to his own people, says, "We kill because our lives and the lives of others lack meaning." A harrowing Nahuatl poem, full of conundrums about the new gods brought by the conquistadors, says, "Our gods have died. Must we die now too?" A popular song from the 16th century goes, "We all leave our bodies, be it today or tomorrow." And a popular saying from the same era: "The poor man always smells of death."

According to Monsiváis, human sacrifice was not only practiced during the time of the Aztecs, but the cruelty continued into the time of the viceroys and, later, of the presidents. In 1968, university students were massacred in Tlatelolco, as were university employees, who were confused with protesters. People have even lost their lives converting to Protestantism.

One topic in particular has shaken up Mexico and Latin America these days: forty-three teachers from a rural district of Guerrero were killed at the hands of police, who were taking orders from the mayor's office. The police delivered them to the narcos, and the narcos made their bodies disappear. In a Guadalajara newspaper, one good article on the subject covers the attitude of President Peña Nieto: "Alchemical and visionary, Doctor Peña Nieto posits that these misfortunes are an extraordinary opportunity to improve the system." The president also spoke of "looking toward the future" (translation: let's forget what happened). Much later on, after mounting tensions from the public and on the advice of his PR team, he sent his heartfelt condolences to the families of the victims. But at the first opportunity, he washed his hands of all responsibility and said that the matter was municipal in nature.

TELEVISION

In Mexico City, I watch a journalist who, to tell certain truths – to differentiate from the official discourse, that is – acts like a clown. He wears a long curly green wig, a red nose, and paints his cheeks white. He moves in long strides and mentions, as if in secret, something about the murder of the rural teachers or the president's contradictions. The clown's got a lot of listeners; the waiter watching him on the TV says, "He says things few others do." But why must he dress up like a clown to do so? Could it have something to do with what

Monsiváis says about the pretense of Mexicans: is it that he's hiding under a clown mask to go unnoticed?

The Ibero-American Summit was going on in Veracruz during those days and every Latin American president was there with the exception of Argentina, Brazil, Venezuela, and Cuba. At no moment do I hear those significant absences being acknowledged; they only show the president pronouncing opening statements, welcoming the King of Spain and Rajoy, the Spanish prime minister, idle politicians in their country. Another TV channel broadcasts that teachers from the state of Guerrero have threatened to interfere in the municipal elections because the candidates have ties with the narcos. Fifteen municipalities are seized and declared a government by those in power. And this important news story is not analyzed or commented upon, it's glossed over like any other topic.

But I'd be lying if I said there weren't any interesting programs. Students of the polytechnic schools were occupying around twenty of their colleges. Seated around a large roundtable, they were directing their questions and demands to the head director of the colleges, accompanied by a lackey who seemed to be in the role of adviser – he didn't speak to the young people.

The kids were denouncing various things: 1) the corrupt heads of the colleges; 2) the practice of nepotism and appointment of relatives who were not fit for positions at the colleges; 3) a director who had cut off their water supply during one occupation; 4) the revenge threats they had received from the authorities in question. Since the students had agreed, conditionally, to cease occupation, based on things like make-up courses to recover lost time, etc., this question arose: To whom do we return the schools? To those same corrupt, nepotistic directors who threatened us? The director of the polytechnic schools said that he would assign a neutral overseer at each college. The students also demanded that the death of a classmate be investigated; she had died during the protests. The general director accepted the majority of their demands, but he asked for more time; meanwhile, the students wanted quick answers. It seemed like he wanted more time so that some of the demands would go away. Many students, for example, wanted the names of corrupt and inept officials to come to light. He refused this demand, basing his decision on protecting the safety of the officials involved. Secrecy, caution, delay, the director had learned these things throughout his life. And those young people, always polite, I might add, demanding their rights. In my view, the fact that they demanded a few things at once worked against the effectiveness of their claims. Each student asked for two or three things, which resulted in the director accepting some demands, postponing others, and rejecting others still. Straightforward questions would have resulted in more direct replies, but now we're getting into distinct cultural norms, where communication isn't always direct.

In return for de-occupying the schools, they also requested the presence of a human rights lawyer. At this request, the director leaned on the excuse that it was difficult to find a civil servant. Who would want to come, who would be available, etc. He must have thought: "These damn kids, always making a scene. Who do they think they are, wanting a human rights lawyer at a time like this?"

THE ARTISAN MARKET

This is how Bernal Díaz del Castillo, chronicler of the Indies, describes an Aztec market from the 16th century:

> In the great marketplace, there are gold and silver wares, feathers, cotton clothing, tiger hides, roots, medicines, otter pelts, venison and mountain lion, legumes, chickens, fruits, honey, and delicacies. Tables, cribs, benches.

In short, a whole neighborhood.

The Aztec marketplace was a massive plaza made up of courtyards, just like the library where I'm reading and the artisan market nearby. The Library of Mexico is one of the largest in the city and has a sequence of hallways and rooms (reading rooms, relaxation rooms, concert halls, etc.), inconspicuous at first glance, which is to say, it's a quietly enormous place. The library does not have a roof, it's open air, for the most part, and is exposed when you get to the outer courtyards. Could it be for the same reason that some pre-Hispanic buildings didn't have ceilings, to make contact with the heavens? It is a little cold inside. The size of the library overwhelms me and I go to the artisan market.

The market must have more than a thousand stalls. Bags, tablecloths, table runners, paintings on bark paper with drawings of flowers and birds of all colors. Other paintings depict scenes from daily life; they are like stories told with small figures, carrying on the tradition of pre-Hispanic pictographic language. There are those beautiful dresses and blouses with embroidered necklines, red bags, a blood red, and thousands of other things. One vendor tells me that in September, on Mexican Independence Day, all the men dress like charros, and the women vendors, in China Poblana style green, red, and white dresses, their hair braided. In Argentina, the dress for the Creole paisanita is light blue, and so are the jerseys of soccer players representing the country.

La Catrina (the afterlife) is at the market too, with her skull face and her dress, black as night with gold embroidery – she is very elegant in her fur stole. There are bags with Frida Kahlo's effigy. I ask a vendor something and he says, "híjoles!" It's an interjection. In one column, a kitsch decoration: an altarpiece of the Virgin of Guadalupe with a helmet of armor beside her; it's under a glass bell, together with some snails. Cribs of all shapes and sizes. In another stall, run by indigenous owners or managers, one woman cooks while the other sews, and a father checks his little girl's calculations. She's about eight years old.

The father looks at her work and says, "It's all wrong."

And the girl buries her head in her hands.

I became tired of looking at one object after the other. I want to take everything or nothing at all, wandering around the stalls like that makes me dizzy. I head to a café.

THE SCHOOL OF SOCIAL ANTHROPOLOGY

The School of Social Anthropology is a one-hour cab ride from my hotel. The driver told me that, during Christmas, people eat buns with chocolate, raisins, and chili. He says: "This custom comes from our ancestors." He also told me that, in general, Mexicans do not turn to psychiatric drugs when they get depressed, but to alcohol.

We arrive at the college, a square and very wide-set building; in the street, food stalls with cooked vegetables, soups, beans, corn tortillas, sweets.

Beside the entrance area, a memorial: forty-three student desks, the ones with built-in tables and chairs, all of them empty, and a large portrait of a teacher who died in Guerrero. Above, a board with the message:

Not terrorists or delinquents
We are all AYOTZINAPA

And below another large board:

All of us are missing

Inside the building, a leaflet on the wall:

Where is Paulino Martínez?
One hundred years since his disappearance

He was a journalist. The poster also announces a funeral without a body, a performance, live music and poetry for Paulino Martinez, who died a hundred years ago.

I wanted to get a coffee, so I had to go down a floor, still slightly limping. There I found a young man with an intelligent face, but no coffee in sight; it was on an upper floor. I asked if he might bring me one and he went flying up the stairs and came back to the little tables on the ground floor, coffee in hand. I started chatting with him. He's an anthropology student named Uziel; he tells me that he comes from a devout family and that his name is biblical. He has a little four-year-old girl, Lilita. "She's named after Adam's first wife," he tells me.

We talk about the disappeared students and he says, "Democracy here is more a pseudo-democracy, human rights organizations issue statements but, in reality, they don't have any power. Some theorists talk about domestic colonialism; indigenous people are not recognized as equals here. People use derogatory words for the poor. 'Macuarro' which means 'construction worker,' is an insult."

He adds: "The narco phenomenon is not an isolated event, it has to do with state-sanctioned terrorism. This school is very politically engaged and we debate two lines of action in our assemblies, the way of pacifism and the way of force. I believe we need to think more deeply, work harder at solving the problems before protesting, so that not everything turns into sheer frenzy."

Level-headed, smart, and cool, all of these qualities in the body of a seventeen-year-old, though he did mention he was twenty-five.

Later I slowly made my way up to the central patio, passing by a man with the face of a Spanish professor. Sure enough, he was, but he was Chilean, exiled after being dismissed by Pinochet. He was completely

Mexicanized: when some of his students would notice him on the patio, he would greet them warmly with "ándale" and "órale." At least ten students go by, and each encounter is festive. I show him a letter from my publisher that authorizes me to interview people, to see if it might convince him to take me to a quieter and shadier room but no, it's clear that he likes to sit in the flower patch. The sun hits me straight on, and I use one hand to shield my face while taking notes with the other. He doesn't seem to be affected by my authorization note and I start to ask him, without enthusiasm, if he thinks what Monsiváis says is true, about the Mexican characteristic of dissimulation.

He says, "In the central region of the country, speaking out against authority figures used to cost people their necks; Mexican courtesy is a little exaggerated – it's linked to the courtly tradition of submission." Since I didn't manage to get much out of that professor – when I'd ask him about some particularity that had stood out to me, he'd answer, "Same as everywhere." I asked instead what had stood out to him when he first arrived.

And he said, "What stood out were the colors of clothes, because they came from before, from the pre-Hispanic era. Don't forget that the Teotihuacan pyramids were painted red, green, yellow, vivid colors. We don't have fashion trends here, each person dresses as they wish, it's not like Argentina or Chile."

And he adds, "Another thing that stood out was that people would invite friends over by saying 'let's get together at your place.'" (which is like saying *mi casa es su casa*.) "There were a lot of Argentine psychoanalysts here, and I used to call them 'airline graduates' because they hadn't followed through with a degree but still practiced."

I mention that the university is very politically engaged and he says, "Yes, we offer housing to students who come to Mexico City from Chiapas."

A student began fawning over him, so I seized the opportunity and left.

A RURAL ANTHROPOLOGIST

I'm in one of the little offices at the college when an assistant finds a man for me to interview. Dark-skinned with black eyes, a short-brimmed hat; evidently, an older man, but his face shows no signs of his age, his skin is smooth and firm as a ripe fruit.

The assistant tells me, "He's a rural anthropologist."

His name is Isidro Sosa and he says, "I like my name because it's short."

It seems to me that he's not ready to answer my questions – he prefers to interview me instead. Eyes smiling, he offers up some generalization to fill the silence, and his laughing eyes are the most playful I've ever seen. I imagine he must be thinking, "Such a long

way just to interview me – let's see how confused this gringa gets."
He asks me things about my past travels and laughs at everything.
And I get the sense that his laugh is a reply like any other.

To return to the hotel, I use two buses, a subway, take a short cab
ride, and walk four blocks. On the bus I sit beside two people eating
something out of a Tupperware container; the young man to my
right is eating salad, he's a social psychologist, the woman on the
other side is having pasta in white sauce. I offer them some fruit
caramels for dessert.

The woman sees that I am a foreigner with a limp and says to me,
"I'll accompany you to the metro."

I resist, she insists, and she guides me to the subway.

While we were riding I asked, "Is it much farther?"

"No," she said, "Only eight stops."

"Only," I thought. I got off at the Zócalo since I already knew how
to negotiate the cab price from there.

I was dropped off at the start of Antonio Caso Street and I couldn't
believe that I needed to walk four blocks to get to 83, even though I'd
done it before. While walking I saw people eating on the sidewalk,
some workers by the looks of it, sitting under a canopy in very formal
chairs. It was like a lounge, but outside.

On the verge of flying home, I remember the Guadalajara Book Fair. In general, when fairs are large, the activities of their participants take place between their hotels and the venue. They go from one to the other, once or twice per day. If any time is left over, it's used to escape. Why? To get to know the city, or to go outside for some fresh air, somewhere by a window, where you can sit and watch people pass by. Somewhere with an inside and an outside, because the fair doesn't have an inside and an outside, it's a self-contained world, in every sense: the bathroom is on Mars, yet inside the building, and you don't meet up with people but bump into them whether you like it or not.

In the case of my hotel in Guadalajara being so spread-out, its rooms so far from the reception, it was also a self-contained world where writers, journalists, and editors would greet each other in passing, with some word of acknowledgment, like ants that barely pause when they're marching in opposite directions. If the person (writer) was not one of our beloved saints, we would choose a roundabout route to avoid greeting them; if the run-in couldn't be avoided, the greeting would happen from a distance. It's possible to communicate, through gestures and body language, that you are in a hurry.

In such open spaces like the hotel, closed spaces, like the fair, and imposing ones, like both of them, run-ins, meetings, and the act of parting ways are understood differently from the usual. If you plan to meet someone and they don't show up, or they get lost along the way, it seems natural. Nearby, there are several people chatting at a table; you can go there, if you'd like, what difference does it make if it's Pedro or Diego. And it's not all about the literary, some people would call Buenos Aires three times a day because of something they lost – it's a fair of desires, possibilities, chance events. An editor told me that she couldn't sleep at the fair and was living in a permanent state of fatigue; a journalist went to explore the city by bus and became enchanted by a shirt and a pair of cheap pants; another spent her free time trying to exchange some damp or flimsy dollars that her boyfriend's mother had stored under a flowerpot.

Another writer showed up with an enormous and heavy package and I said, "What do you have there?"

"A mask, it's a gift for my sister."

It was the effigy of an evil god that weighed about twenty kilograms. Where would her sister put it? Another writer arrived around seven hours later than everyone. She was furious: she'd been detained at the Mexico City airport because they had discovered a packet of yerba mate in her luggage. There's at least one flight daily between Buenos Aires and Mexico City. Do they really need six hours to determine whether there's drugs in the yerba? Anyway.

I also thought of my guardian angels and the three heavy books I'd given to them as gifts, short story anthologies from the fair; if I am certain of one thing, it's that I prefer not to carry my burdens, but rather to unburden myself.

AIRPORT

If the Guadalajara fair is monumental, and the hotel property too, the Mexico City airport gives them both a run for their money. All of the employees are wearing Santa hats, and I receive a sour young man as my TSA screener. He had a face that said "get away from me," and he kept readjusting his hat, which was falling from his head, becoming more furious by the moment. While going through customs, they took a mini bottle of tequila from me because it violated some law or other. And I didn't look for anything else to buy because I had one foot in Buenos Aires; the foot hit the ground when a literary critic I knew by name came over to me. We were on the same flight. It was like we were back in Guadalajara. I lost her when I boarded (airport relationships are similar to the ones at hotels and book fairs; people lose each other on the jet bridge to the airplane – if they reunite inside, good, if not, it's in God's hands).

Losing track of her suited me because I wasn't ready to land in Buenos Aires yet; stray memories were coming back to me: the squirrel thieves from Chapultepec Park who would steal the stall vendors' spiced chocolate and kiosk signs that said "Natural Tamarind Candy with Salt and Chili Pepper." And a liquid: Sangría Señorial. I remembered the guide from the Museum of Anthropology, old and severely limping, who was leading a long tour, going up and down the stairs. "I'm used to it," she said. She was sanctimonious and didn't stop in front of any phallic symbols because her religion didn't allow it, and would say things like: "A planetary conjunction of several planets made possible the birth of God's son." And the museum itself was so impressive that it challenged the ignorance or intelligence of any guide.

I remembered a woman who was cleaning the hotel. She said of my sandals, "Those huaraches must be so comfortable."

But then the memories stopped; María Teresa Andruetto, a Cordoban writer I know, was in the row beside mine. She came up to me for a chat and we talked about her house in Villa Allende, which I'd been to, and where she keeps a donkey and several sheep. And suddenly we were elsewhere, in Argentina.

A QUESTION OF BELONGING

THE FIRST TIME I WENT to La Paz, despite being very young, I was affected by the altitude. I felt as though I had a thick soup inside my head. It is not a disagreeable sensation, but a strange one, as if you are turning into someone else. As if you are entering another dimension. What's more, I had to walk slowly because the streets of La Paz rise and fall and it's easy to get worn out. I saw people pass by carrying bundles of grass, sticks of ice, and bags of firewood that caused them to lean over as they walked. Many of them were young and already hunched from carrying so many things on their backs. My altitude sickness suddenly seemed less important, so I thought: Why can't they just carry everything in a little cart? And I imagined one for them, made all of wood, even the wheels. The next day I visited a cathedral and noticed a sign beside the baptismal font: "It is prohibited to throw confetti and tissue paper inside the temple." Seeing as I didn't know anything about popular religious customs back then, or the mixing of rituals, I thought, "Who in their right mind would throw tissue paper inside a church?" I considered the reasons they might have for throwing tissue paper. Could it be that the priests of La Paz had some screws loose?

What was apparent, however, were the number of people begging, or that were bowlegged from malnourishment, so I again imagined a means for everyone to be fed. It would have to involve a religious ceremony, a ritual. The chosen one, preferably dressed in white, would climb to the top of a hill and from there emerge to bless the food and command: "Let us now drink the milk! Spread the honey! Eat the bread!"

I also noticed that people did not look each other in the eye. They would keep their heads lowered or look into the distance, as if passing through the other person, which made me think: They must have their own way of looking. I bought a Quechua-Spanish dictionary, where the expression "mirar de soslayo," to look sideways, had more than twenty synonyms.

Later we went to Tiahuanaco, a sacred site, and we must have missed the bus on the way back because two rural men gave us a ride in the bed of their truck. Neither of them spoke Spanish. We offered them a few oranges and they gave us a blanket because it was freezing. Just like that, using only smiles, we were able to understand each other. And I learned that it is not necessary to speak to understand one another. Some other day (again I can't remember how we got there or met these people) we went to some offices in the middle of the desert. A couple drove us in their car; he was Bolivian and she North American. Supposedly, the office was a help center for indigenous people.

They invited us to a meal at the center. He was an engineer, a handsome mestizo, and she, the leader of the troops, was an ashen blonde. She must have been a fourth-tier secretary in her home country, but in La Paz she bossed people around with the vigor of a resurrected louse. He yielded to her. She badmouthed the Indians – I remember her saying that, despite having taught them to use cutlery, they would eat with their hands as soon as they were left alone. I would have done the same, I thought, if I had been used to eating with my hands, but there wasn't room to argue or disagree with her. He nodded along to everything she said. Each comment was a complaint about the Indians' behavior. It is very difficult to intervene in a speech without cracks.

The second time I went to La Paz, I was young, thirty something, and better read when it came to politics and the rest. I got altitude sickness then, too. I was already a little nervous by the time I arrived at the airport and saw a kind of first aid station where people were being tended to. I asked about the station and they told me it was for patients with asthma and heart problems. I sensed the altitude, that same feeling of soup inside my head, but it was nothing new this time. Still, I spent the first two days lying in bed. Altitude sickness is benign, in a way, because it's not like one is lying there unable to bear it – one desires nothing in this state. On the third day, I visited Soria, the screenwriter of Sanjinés's Blood of the Condor. (Speaking of that excellent director, I saw his film on Evo Morales, a compelling story in which Evo is depicted not as some kind of miracle, but instead as a result of countless peasant uprisings. At the end of the 19th century, the peasants, instead of fleeing from the army's gunfire, kept right on advancing; the army did not cease their killing and they did not cease their marching.)

Soria was available to meet right away. Burly, dark-haired, and smiling, he told me how they used to resort to nonprofessional actors because there hadn't been enough to go around. At that time, the same actors who did theater also did film, no more than ten or twelve of them. His film tells the story of a U.S. agency that was allegedly assisting women with childbirth, until the husbands found out that each time their wives went there, their children would die. They would also sterilize the women without their consent. Soria told me that they screened the film in many communities throughout the country – some people who had never stepped foot inside a cinema went to go see it. The film was made up of raccontos, but they switched to linear time to make it easier to follow. Soria dislocated his ankle during one shoot in the mountains, and they took care of him within the community; when he reached La Paz, he sought medical attention. He used both medicines, the one from the mountains and the one he got in the city. He recounted all of this with humility, patience, and a smile.

A little while ago, I had a strong desire to return to La Paz, to see how things were going with Evo Morales, but I was afraid of the four thousand meters. So I thought, Argentina has so many communities, in La Plata, Escobar, Liniers, and Morón, I could just visit one a bit closer to home. And so I did. One Sunday, I took a bus to Once, a train to Morón, another bus to the Morón military air base, and then walked three blocks. The neighborhood was like many others on the outskirts of the city; asphalt roads, a motorbike parked out front in the little garden, the occasional car. Some dogs were awake but the owners of the building were asleep because it was early (I always arrive early, wherever I go). I didn't see any signs of the Bolivian community. I was hoping for a whole neighborhood, and I asked the only neighbor who was awake where the community was.

He said, "Ring the bell out front, everyone's inside."

It turned out not to be a neighborhood, but a chapel where mass was celebrated the first and third Sunday of each month, followed by lunch, and this is where people from the community, who came from elsewhere, converged. My point of contact with the community was Beba, but I hadn't met her in person yet.

"Are you staying for lunch?" she asked on the phone.

Yes, I said with enthusiasm, thinking of the loads of questions I had prepared: How did she feel when she first arrived in Argentina, what did she miss about home, etc. Right beside the chapel was a local spot where I was waited on by the manager. From what I could tell, she seemed part of the Bolivian community – I told her that I was waiting for Beba. She looked at me with deep-seated distrust and almost didn't let me in, the only reason I was able to slip by was because the gatekeeper's son-in-law came in.

I asked him, "Excuse me, are you part of the community?"

"No, but my mother-in-law is."

Before going in, I glanced at the signs hanging on the front door. An engraving above me read: "Community of Bolivian residents, Our Lady of Copacabana." Below: "Drinks are prohibited inside the church." And a third sign, to protect against theft, extortion, and phone scams. The header: "How do I answer unknown callers?" Several scenarios were provided. One of the prompts was: "We are watching you." Response: "What color is my shirt?" It's clear they were a cautious people.

When I went in, I observed the place – it was spacious enough for dances and all kinds of events, with wooden benches and tables and bathrooms at the back that had signs in Spanish and Quechua.

The kitchen was off to one side. I told the cook why I was there; she hadn't heard of Beba either.

She said, "Talk to the manager, you won't get anything but chatter from me."

Cars were beginning to pull up, some of them important, and I approached an older man who got out with his wife and two granddaughters.

I said, "Are you part of the community, sir?"

"No, but my wife is."

His wife had already gone in and he led me into the chapel, where there was a small, but very pretty icon of the Virgin of Copacabana. He also led me to the sacristy which had a display case with lots of dresses inside.

"What's with the dresses?"

"They belong to the Virgin. She has over 35 of them."

I noticed that some had silver trim, another had the Argentine coat of arms on the sleeve, plenty of green and gold. The shelf above held the Virgin's crowns, which appeared to be made of silver. His wife was in the chapel with their granddaughters.

She told the girls, "You must pray to the Virgin."

To set an example, she prayed out loud: "Our Lady of Copacabana, give me the strength and courage to stand up to my enemies who humiliate and diminish me."

I left the chapel because I felt as though I was intruding. I thought to myself: "People who have enemies are (or think they are) important. They won't answer any of my questions."

I saw a woman with indigenous features beside the door and she said to me, "Interview my husband, he's right there."

He was happy to lend his time, but his wife vanished. We sat down on a bench in the lobby while a woman lingered behind us, as though she wanted to join in. She had indigenous features and was well dressed, in city clothes.

I said, "Please join us."

We sit down in the big assembly hall and I begin my interview.

The man says, "Oh, but I'm Spanish, I'm not native."

Joking, I say, "So you're of no use to me."

I asked the other woman, who had slipped into the conversation and who had indigenous features, if she was native.

She said, "Me, not one bit."

She said that all of her grandparents had been Spanish. So I wrapped up the interview and stood by the door, waiting for more people to arrive. I approached a couple who seemed to be from different ethnic groups and asked them the same old question.

"No," said the woman, visibly annoyed. Her husband wavered as though he wanted to stay behind and talk to me a little, but she said, "Let's go, let's go" and took him with her.

Defeated, I went to see if the famous Beba had arrived. I found her at a very busy moment – she was checking people's names off a spreadsheet, possibly for a future trip to Tucumán that was advertised on a sign above the chapel door.

Beba said, "Many of them come from native communities, but they aren't going to say so because they don't want to be taken for country folk. They're going to deny it. Are you staying for lunch?"

"No, thank you, my stomach's been bothering me."

And I left, whistling softly.

CORRIENTES CASTS A SPELL

B EFORE DEDICATING MYSELF almost exclusively to writing travelogues, I wrote a few that got lost. Two or three were published; the one that I'm trying to remember now came out in a magazine, and that magazine wasn't reprinted, so it seemed right that the story should disappear too. I threw it away during a move and it was as if it had never existed. I liked listening to chamamé at the time and would stand still when "Kilómetro once" was playing, as though it were the national anthem. I bought a record by a folk artist from Corrientes whose name I don't remember. In one song, he explains to his son how to best lead one's life, saying things like: "Respect authority, but don't let them chase you down." What follows is a string of advice that, to me, encompasses everything you need to know about getting by in the world.

A journalist friend of mine said, "Go and write the story, but we don't have money to pay you." In truth, I could have paid three times what I paid to go to Corrientes on that janky bus, but I had to save money for a hotel and wanted to stay for as many days as possible. I went during the summer because I didn't want to wait for winter. "Wait till winter!" people would tell me, and "What is with you and chamamé, do you have a Correntino relative or something?" I didn't care one bit that it was summer, I was ready to go right away. There was a gaucho on the bus, dressed head to toe in traditional clothes, hat and all. I interpreted his presence as a sign of my journey's success, and I sat down beside him. We started talking.

"What's it like there?"

"Over there," he said, "no one drinks Fernet or Gancia." He had a lisp. "They'll sooner order a caña. They're in the middle of a crotera right now, my child..."

I held on to that word, "crotera," and would use and abuse it when the financial crisis made its way to Buenos Aires. Later we talked about Don Montiel and Tránsito Cocomarola and I didn't get up out of respect for the gaucho, who was a very measured man. When night came, I went to sleep in the empty seats in the back; in the morning I returned to my seat beside him, reclaiming my spot. But it was clear that I had offended him by leaving his side in the first place and he treated me coldly. Looking back, I think he may have had a reason to take offense, because I moved around that rundown bus like I owned the place – perhaps he thought that a person should remain in the place that destiny had assigned them.

When I arrived at my hotel room (a dark and sad room, but I didn't care at all), a maid was making the bed.

"Did you hear about the bus accident yesterday? Twelve girls from the Ara Berá troupe died. I'm with Copacabana, but a girl from Ara Berá was my neighbor, so I went to the wake anyway." (Copacabana was Ara Berá's arch nemesis.)

I thought that this was a singular explanation and that unusual things were in store for me.

I don't remember having any Buenos Aires connections there, but I must have had one because the first person I talked to was a Buenos Aires psychoanalyst now based in Corrientes. We met one afternoon for a whiskey and he told me things about his patients. "In Buenos Aires, the upper class goes to therapy to prevent information leaks, here it's the middle class that goes to therapy – students, young lawyers." He added, "And whoever my patient is, whatever the reason for their visit, I do not start a session without asking if someone's cast a spell on them, a payé."

"What do you mean?" I said.

"You see, the patient will be curled up on the corner of the divan and won't talk about what's going on with them until I say, 'Have you received a payé?' They always say yes, and then we calmly begin with Oedipus, Elektra, the usual."

I said goodbye to the psychoanalyst, stepped out into the street (it was midday), and just then I remembered the warnings about summer and my ancestors on both sides. The whiskey merged with the sun to cast a payé on me and I thought I might dissolve in the middle of the street. Luckily this didn't happen and I sought shade at my sad hotel, and in the evening, now restored, I went for a tour of the city, peeking into all of the residential courtyards. I saw lemon trees, orange blossoms, colorful flowers, and it gave me the feeling that the intimate part of a house was not in its rooms, but its courtyards.

I saw a woman who looked like she knew her way around and asked her, "Señora, which way is downtown?"

She gave a haughty reply, "Downtown is over there." (Stressing the ll in allá) "Now if you'd like more of a downtown . . ."

I took this to mean that if I wanted a more bustling city then I should go back to where I came from. I hadn't yet read about the motives of the bad blood between Correntinos and Porteños; this bad blood had started before the Paraguay War. When the war was declared, the Correntinos did not want to go. They used to say, "Porteño and serpent on the cross, one and the same." I attributed a regional and exotic character to the woman's reply.

. . . . . .

Later I interviewed an architect who was the head organizer of the carnival troupes.

He said, "How did you get here? Oh, by bus. Poor journalist. Here carnival is organized a year in advance and I receive funds from the Department of Culture. The director is my brother-in-law; last year, I confronted him and said, 'Give me money for the carnival.' He told me they didn't have any, but I persisted until I wore him down. He's a little guy, but he stood up like he was tall and said, very solemnly, 'I am now speaking to you as the Director of Culture.'"

The brother-in-law director had to go to Buenos Aires for a hip operation, so the architect told him, "Seeing as you refuse to give me money for the carnival, I'm going to cast a payé on you – let's see if you ever walk again."

"So he gave me the money. How could anything have been organized, if not for me? Costumes, floats, lights."

Since I was stunned by all of that passion for the carnival, he went on, "When their favorite troupes lose, some people throw bottles at the television, or splash the judges with soda; there's a lot of them from Buenos Aires, the dance judges come from Colón, some are for visual arts and sculptures, and a handful of other categories. They're put up in separate hotels to make sure their votes aren't influenced. Once, the public didn't like the panel's vote, so they pelted the judges with oranges on their way to the airport."

I do remember the architect giving me the address of a woman whose daughter was the carnival queen the year before. Their house was quintessentially middle class, the decorations too, but with one particularity: instead of spending money on painting it a little better, they'd spent money on building a room to exhibit the queen's dress. An entire room, just for a dress. The woman was aware of her role as the queen's mother; I mentioned the deaths of the Ara Berá girls. "Mhm, we are with Copacabana." And she judiciously expressed her condolences.

That is what I remember. I always wanted to return to Corrientes, but since I could only do so in the summer and age accentuated my prudence, I didn't go back.

NEW YEAR'S IN ALMAGRO

CHRISTMAS AND NEW YEAR'S awaken altruistic feelings in me. I am reminded of the people in the world who grow up, suffer, and die, and I cease to think of myself as the center of the universe – the "cake filling" as they say in Cuyo and Chile. This altruism has a certain poetic uselessness, but I manage to give it meaning. I am aware of the many people in the city without electricity, and others who go without gas or a roof over their heads. I don't do anything to help them. How could I manage to fix all of their problems? But if I am going to dinner at an expensive restaurant, like Las Violetas, for example, I first take a dip in the seedy dive bar out front, where I have a coffee. That way, I won't be affected by the wealth of the restaurant.

The bar has a sort of veranda with little wooden tables where you can smoke – tables that were never touched by the hand of God. The coffee tastes like rat poison; a pale, sallow woman who looks like she's made more than a few rash life decisions sits in front of me, drinking a cup. The bathrooms are down a pitch-black hallway. One single red light illuminates the bar – it does not seem to signal fun and merriment, but danger. The dive bar is the most anti-New Year's place there is, but on December 31st at 8:30 p.m. it becomes significant to me, because of my altruistic feelings. The bathroom door is covered in pornographic sketches, filthy not for what they show, but for their crude strokes. The bathroom itself is a subhuman bachelor pad. It reminds me of what Empedocles once said: "Fish live in a monad where not a ray of intelligence shines in." Same goes for the signs. One says: "Don't forget the door, don't forget your whore." This doesn't quite add up, since whoever wrote it won't be leaving, not ever – it's the bathroom succubus. Two police officers come in and it's clear they are friends with the owner who greets them from behind the bar: "Happy New Year, girls." One of the police officers has dyed blonde hair the color of sunflowers. She returns the greeting. The owner says, "Bye girls, have a good night." I remember that it's New Year's Eve and that police officers have houses too, where they will probably go for a shower and a drink.

Sitting at the old wooden table, as though I am on a secluded beach and the table has known sunlight and breezes, I watch people pass by. I notice they are leaving their houses and heading for other destinations – some have bags or little shopping carts in tow; others are dressed up for a visit, carrying gifts. Some are simply in flip flops, taking their dogs for one last walk before giving them calming drops of medicine to deal with the racket of New Year's. The bar pulses with the beat of cumbia villera and I remember the signs and drawings on the walls that are like hooked arabesques. Why do they keep it so dark inside the bar? Why is it only lit up by the occasional candle, as though more would be too stimulating? Who would dwell in such a place? Incubi and succubi.

By now it's time to have a drink and eat dinner at Las Violetas. I have passed through hell and I deserve a drink with my friends. The emperor penguin at Las Violetas, who never greets anyone and always looks me up and down, does not greet me. Getting annoyed is not an option: it's New Year's. And the waiters glide backwards and forwards, dancing as though they are back in the Belle Époque. They uncork bottles here and there, in synchronized harmony, and the only thing missing is a Viennese waltz. We talk about Paris, London, and Ireland, and I say what I always do, that I would like to visit Ireland and Portugal because they are small places and easy to navigate. But I'm not certain that I would go now, because it's New Year's, and I like being in my neighborhood. My friend's husband says that the world is as small as a handkerchief and that he bumped into somebody he knew in London. It's true, I think, the world is a handkerchief, but a giant one. I am reminded of a painting I saw by some artist or other; it was of all the little windows of an apartment building and you could see a woman sitting in a chair inside one of them, someone watering plants in another – each person doing something different.

Yes, it's all well and good in places like Paris, London, and elsewhere, but something at the neighboring table catches my attention: two men, one of whom is older, but not by much, and a younger man who doesn't seem to have anything in common with him. The older one seems grateful for his luck; he looks like a salesman, with a good-natured face, one of those guys who flies under the radar but gets what he wants without making a fuss. He's probably thinking, "Luckily I can afford this meal at Las Violetas. It's hard to believe that I'm here, I who..." The younger one looks like he studies something cerebral, like philosophy. His knowledge casts a shadow over his eyes and forehead – surely he must be thinking that everything around him is a display of vanity. What is the glue that holds them together? They do not seem related, or like they could be friends. Yet another mystery of New Year's Eve. And it's New Year's for those in Antarctica, for beggars and thieves.

The next day, everything is closed except the corner store. The owner, a Chinese man, is a friend of mine.

"Are you really open today?" I say.

"Chinese New Year is on January 31st."

"Oh. Any plans to celebrate?"

"A little bit," he says. His smile accentuates the shine of his eyes. "Yes, with pineapple soda."

THE NORTH AMERICAN PROFESSOR

WHEN SPRING ARRIVES in the north and swallows migrate northward, North American literature professors migrate down here. A professor from California comes to visit. She is polite as the rest of them and says, as expected, that she is not from Los Angeles or any other city we've heard of. Her university is in a small town, 10,000 inhabitants, give or take. I suggest that this number is underwhelming, what we Porteños might call a shithole.

"Oh no," she says, "I am very happy with my work, students, and friends."

I can tell she is middle-aged, but also a real-life example of "piel de manzana." Her hair is flawless, freshly washed, short and silky (I've noticed that none of them wear it curly). I am on the verge of a terrible outburst: I want to ask how she takes care of her hair and what kind of brush she uses, but I decide to ask her something more civilized.

"How advanced are your students?"

"Oh, not very. They don't read."

"They plan to teach literature and they don't read?"

It could be that they don't read, or that they do read but don't understand, or that they do understand but don't know how to express themselves.

I take the opportunity to complain a little about our students and she shakes her head, "I don't know how they will manage their own lives or families later."

"Sure," I say. But I had never thought of that – here everyone manages to carry on with their lives and families however they want, or are able to.

With respect to the students, she adds, "But they are good people, oh."

What had she wanted to say? That they do not steal, or kill, or behave unpredictably during class time? I take for granted that my students are good people. Considering she is so honest, maybe she thinks it's wrong to criticize someone in their absence, and this is a shame: I would have liked to hear about the particularities of her students. The tone in which she says "good people," along with her pristine appearance, leads to a hiatus in the conversation. On the one hand, I feel as though I am in the company of the Korean woman from a Juana Molina sketch, and on the other, with the living image of the Puritan empire, despite the fact that one of her earrings is much bigger than the other. Her disregard for the earring and her attitude toward work cause the earring's large size to be less noticeable – it becomes symmetrical, harmonious even. It does not hang on her; rather, she wears it. Luckily she mentioned her cat, for whom she had organized some casual festivities.

I too have a cat. It is striking to see how he mimics my guests: he sniffs her shoes, of course, but his sniff is prudent and cautious. Never has my cat smelled the shoes of a North American professor with reckless abandon, the way he might sniff certain people who seem cautious and prudent themselves. Who knows why, but he rushes toward some coat, dives into it, and disappears. It is common knowledge that North Americans love animals (maybe they feel they must since they extended human rights to them), but this suits me because it means that I won't feel obliged to lock my cat into a room, like I do when hosting certain Argentine guests who are afraid or intolerant of cats or demand that mine get off the table.

I am unable, at this point, to hold in another outburst: "What do you feed your cat?"

"Oh, special food, meat and tomatoes."

Of course, all North American cats must have special tins of food. Mine does not, because I reject cultural dependency. I don't make this joke out loud because it would be difficult to explain. I notice that when she says "oh," she means to say "of course," or something along those lines. If I could translate the meaning of that North American "oh," I would succeed in learning English. Their "oh" is very different from our "ah." Our "ah" is an "ah, now I get it," an expression of courtesy or sympathy. To me, their "oh" sounds like an affirmation that the world is marching as it should, and no other way. She has made it to my apartment without getting lost, and has done so by subway not taxi – not out of frugality, but because she was guided by her own compass – reason – her trusty guide that makes any place, however far away, reachable. After we talked about all of these cute trivialities, I asked her what she thought of Argentines.

She said, "Oh, they're a little cranky, but they told me that before I left."

They had warned her, and she had come prepared.

She took out a tape recorder and a questionnaire she had drafted in advance and asked what the difference was between a story and a narrative. Since I did not know or care to know, I asked her instead. She told me that a narrative was open-ended. I realized I would need to come up with something quickly, so I worked out a theory on the spot about the containedness of stories and the advantages thereof, citing the Greeks and the benefits of the round form, and she seemed to accept my reply. It seemed to me that I would have to define those things in two shakes, otherwise I would never succeed at interviews – how could I if I was indifferent to such things. She called my style "minimalist." I vacillated between knowing what she was trying to say (when I concentrated, I could figure it out) and then later losing interest. This is what happens to us: we learn things and then forget them after a while.

It was another good opportunity to ask what she thought, but I was already thinking about other things, for example if it was appropriate to meet again or to invite her for a drink or meal. In general, North American literature professors do not eat or drink during formal meetings; moreover, she told me that she had some condition of the esophagus that sometimes caused her to choke on her food. It caused a blockage of her internal mechanisms, such that her esophagus would freeze and the food would come back up. I had never heard of this condition.

She said, "Oh, they've found a name for it."

It was progress, without a doubt. This condition that closes the stomach or esophagus brings to mind the advantages and disadvantages of invulnerability. Invulnerability is a beautiful thing and I would go all the way back to the United States to see how I might achieve it – but invulnerability causes our esophagus, or whatever else inside us, to freeze. The esophagus closes up, stubbornly, when people deny themselves every whim and spontaneity.

The conversation about her esophagus petered out. She descends like they all do from Nordic gods; unlike our gods, theirs are not erratic. The North American God or gods have well defined plans: one for the esophagus and another for interviews.

Right then she told me she liked my stories, but that she saw sadness, not happiness in them. She also saw family affection, but not happiness. I could have asked what type of sadness it was, since sadness comes in infinite varieties: sordid, triumphant, heart-wrenching, empty, etc.

But her observation left me speechless, so I said, "I never realized."

She understood and immediately moved on.

I began to understand why North Americans do not wish to live in big, populated cities. Every time I go to a city, regardless of its size, I ask where the center is. Then I saturate myself with the center, with the people who pass by, with the lights and the billboards. I go so that the sadness will dissipate. They do not look for a center because they create centers of their own: there she was, bravely, asking me about sadness and receiving silence in return. She gave me my time and, in the case of no reply, it was on to the next thing.

Just when I was about to ask why North American women were such feminists, she said, "On to something interesting: are women writers different from men?"

Sometimes I think that they are, because they dress differently, spit differently, and hardly any women are plumbers or cockroach exterminators – pest control workers are always men. They also swallow pills in a different way, women grab the little morsel with their fingers, while I've seen men gulp the pill from their open palm. There are special cases of course, exceptions. I didn't explain all of this due to idiomatic differences.

She added, "Are women better at writing about their inner lives?"

"I'd have to see."

Honest and diligent, she said, "I'll have to read more to find out."

After that, she left. The northern swallow, following her radar. She went to the flower shop – she knew that it was near my apartment without checking outside, without having looked left or right, or having seen any sign. And she was on her way.

"I'll have to read more to find out."

After that, she left. The northern swallow, following her radar. She went to the flower shop – she knew that it was near my apartment without checking outside, without having looked left or right, or having seen any sign. And she was on her way.

INSIDE THE CIRCUS

THE PUERTA ROJA THEATER, at 3600 Lavalle Street, exhibits photos, videos, and circus costumes. Members of famous circus families are among the crowd, such as Rivero, Sarrasani, and Shangri-La. The opening of the exhibit was a special occasion – I felt I couldn't miss it. I said to myself: *There are probably four or five photos – I'll do a quick tour, stay for half an hour and, to reward myself for my efforts, grab a coffee somewhere nearby.* But it wasn't just four or five photos, it was a performance featuring old bands (whose cues let the artists know when to enter) and a finale with juggling and rhythmic gymnastics. Most of the circus families in town were there. The families know each other; in some cases they are related, or have married someone from another troupe.

One woman was covering another's eyes and saying, "Guess who?"... "Oh, it's you! I haven't seen you since so-and-so's wedding..."

I was invited by Diana Rutkus, a student from my writing

workshop. Diana was born in the circus. Since she was so busy on opening day, she left me with her mom, a former trapeze artist who used to walk the tightrope with an umbrella. Her mother noticed me looking at a charming photo of her balancing with her umbrella.

"That's me, all right," she says. "Oh, how time ravages us!"

When the band started to play, Diana's mom went inside to cry freely, and I did the same from my seat. Many of us were crying for what was long gone, for the old circus and its animals, when we heard a march that signaled the start of the show. An old musician was playing it – he had played it his entire life, but now he was part of a band. When Diana's mom comes back, she is rejuvenated. She tells me that she gave away all of her costumes after she left the circus – she couldn't bear to look at them anymore. Diana says that her mom, who is over seventy years old, still dresses up as a clown to liven up childrens' parties. Her brother Juan, who is filming the show, spellbound, says that when he walks his two dogs, his mom will sometimes say, "Why don't we do a little shtick with the dogs?"

Juan is two years older than Diana and is able to remember more. They both grew up in the trailer and remember sitting on the floor and watching their mom put on her makeup.

Juan says, "She had a little box that said 'Kaunas Circus' on it with makeup and brushes inside. She always looked radiant. When it was time to remove her makeup, she would let each of us take off a false eyelash."

Juan also remembers when they would go to the parquet together to watch their acrobat mom. Diana was three years old and still used a pacifier – she always had two or three pacifiers with her because she couldn't stand it when the gummy got warm. And their mother, the diva up above, would greet them in some small way, a little wave, a wink, some kind of gesture.

Juan adds, "We would clap for Mom until our hands stung." And: "Nothing reminds me more of childhood than the smell of lipstick."

"I studied architecture," he continues, "and was part of a stage production for *The Seagull*, where I learned to apply makeup perfectly. I always remembered Mom's words: 'There is nothing sweeter than applause – it measures how well you performed.' I used her advice for the theater."

What did they play when they lived at the circus? Circus. They would set up a tent on the double bed in their trailer; Juan was the owner of the circus, Diana and Celeste (their neighbor) the employees. They were also allowed to play inside the real circus. Each family had a unique whistle for calling their kids inside and everyone knew the whistles from other trailers.

Juan says, "To this day, if I'm out walking around Corrientes or Florida and spot someone from the circus, I call out to them with their whistle and they turn around. My dog comes to me when I whistle, but people only turn around because they're not used to it – nobody whistles anymore."

Diana says, "We used to wake up to the roar of lions."

They weren't afraid of them at all.

Juan says: "I used to play with lion cubs, they were my favorite animals to play with – fuzzy, chubby, and solid. I remember their smell. One lioness was called Gesell because my grandpa made friends with Old Man Gesell when he visited the Villa. Our great-grandma told our grandma that she had been friends with Chaplin's mother. Our dad's grandmother used to be Mirtha Legrand's private teacher, but when she left the circus, she felt as though a limb had been cut off. She recovered over time, or so she told people on the outside. When we began telling our high school classmates about all this, they didn't believe us. So for a long time we didn't share anything at all."

When they left the circus, Diana was five and Juan was seven. He had moved schools a few times already, but hadn't interacted much with the outside world.

Diana says, "When I started school I was more afraid of my teachers and classmates than I was of the lions. I was used to the lions because they slept outside our trailer and would wake me in the morning with their roars. Once the teacher asked us to draw our houses and I drew our trailer and some people going into the circus."

Juan says, "School was a hassle because we would move every twenty days. If we fell behind, it was a strain to catch up, and if we were ahead, I would get bored. I remember one school, somewhere around Misiones, I think, that had a piano. I had never seen one before. But what was even more intriguing was the playground, a kind of inner patio that led to other rooms. We had been used to the playground outside our trailer. The first song they taught us on the piano was 'We're invited to tea time.' And I would think about little teacups and kettles. Later I found out that it was by María Elena Walsh."

Their paternal grandfather was Lithuanian; he didn't come from circus origins. During his time as a soldier in World War I, he met a Yugoslav man who taught him calisthenics and handstands. From Hamburg they went to Cuba and traveled around Latin America together as acrobats. They became very well known in Venezuela and the newspapers would announce their arrival far in advance. And not only were they acrobats, but boxers as well – they would challenge locals. He was very adventurous and earned good money boxing and performing calisthenics.

Diana says, "My grandpa bought a circus, he had a fleet of trucks and made a good living, but that was before, when deals were made with a handshake. My dad was born in my grandpa's circus and came from a line of circus owners and my mom worked for the Rivero circus, a typical business where you clocked in and out: one tardy arrival and your payment got docked. My grandpa didn't run his circus like that. He lost everything because he sued the guy who stiffed him. He won the suit, but the guy showed up and said, 'You're robbing me of the only house I've got,' and my grandpa felt sorry for him (he was too kind for his own good) so he had to give up his circus. Mom was born in Brazil, but she was in Uruguay when I was about to be born and she traveled to Buenos Aires so that I could be Argentine. She was no longer able to do trapeze – and what she liked most was to fly – so she had to quit the profession. The problem was that, after washing so many clothes, her hands turned coarse and she couldn't get a tight grip. My grandpa bought a house in Plátanos, he planted trees all along his property, so that's where we went. Mom took a job as a packer in a factory but she couldn't get used to her new job. She missed flying. Dad also started working in a factory and would say, 'We earn less in a month than we used to earn in a week.'"

Juan has a fond memory from those precarious days. Often they would arrive at the entrance of some town at night, a tractor towing their trailers and cages. His mom would wake him up so he could see the lights.

He says, "You could see all of them, as if from an airplane."

After seeing those dazzling lights, he would go back to sleep.

A SUIT WITH AN EXTRA PAIR OF PANTS

A LONG TIME AGO, Atilio and I lived in an apartment that my mom had purchased because he said the last one depressed him so much he couldn't work. He had a point: the elevator in my old building had been jammed for about seventy years. When the windowpane fell onto us, we patched it up with cardboard and resolved to start a new life in a smaller, but newer apartment. I dreamed of decorating it to my taste – I must have had a little taste in me – but I didn't know how people found all those pretty things for their houses. I chose the decorations very carefully since Atilio tended to insult them, trip over or break them. We did save one thing from my old apartment, a small single bed, which I viewed as a discomfort I was destined to endure. At night, he would come home from his meanderings with the same old story: he had gotten into it with a huge military guy wearing epaulets, and had won.

"Go to bed," I would tell him gently, anticipating his speech about mediocre people not knowing the meaning of a heroic gesture.

When I'd leave for work, he'd be sleeping, enveloped in a cloud of alcohol.

"Let's get you cleaned up," I said one day, determined.

We went to see a doctor who prescribed him vitamins, but even his vitamins were different from the rest of the human race's – they were brown and circular, like grainy meatballs. I also took him to a psychiatrist, who he called Dr. Doormat. The session went differently from the way they tend to go. Atilio entered loudly, slurring his words.

Dr. Doormat said, "Shh. Why don't you sit down, nice and calm now."

Given he was afraid of the police, the military, doctors, his girlfriends' mothers, dogs, and traveling, Atilio obeyed. He told me that if he was going to get a job, he would need a new suit, and I wasn't going to let an opportunity like that pass us by. My mom gave me money to go to Casa Muñoz, where one peso was worth two and a suit came with an extra pair of pants. Atilio always wore a suit with a dress shirt and tie – not once did I ever see him in a casual jacket or jeans. Deep down he wanted to fit in, but the odds were stacked against him. He had worked at an insurance company for a few months where, according to some protocol I'd never heard of, he'd been promoted to company secretary. His job was to take the minutes at meetings. But it caused him so much anxiety to write everything down (he couldn't catch even half of what was said) that he threw the minute book into the Riachuelo River. Afterward he was anxious he might be punished and felt humiliated for lying since he told his colleagues he had lost the book.

So I went to Casa Muñoz with the confidence of someone fulfilling an important role, while he waited in the bar on the corner (he always waited in the bar on the corner) for me to carry out my official duties. I didn't have any of his measurements, so I brought a spool of thread to measure the length of the pants – in such a hectic and eventful life, measurements are irrelevant details. I had just gone inside that beautiful shop with its elegant salesmen when it occurred to me that I was going about things all wrong, but I wasn't one to be easily daunted, so I put the spool on the counter.

"Oh, no. This won't do. The young man must come in person."

"He's in the bar on the corner," I said weakly.

"Bring him here."

As though it were an easy feat, I went to convince Atilio and he followed me to the shop, terrified. Two tall, elegantly dressed salesmen were standing by the door, an arrogant air about them. Atilio was skinny and dressed in tattered clothing – he looked at the shop and its giants like he couldn't believe his eyes. The two large and prestigious men took his measurements in a corner.

When we left, one of the giants, a security guard of sorts, said, "You need to eat more, young man, you are too skinny."

I would soon need to return to Casa Muñoz because both pairs fell to disuse. I don't know where the first pants disappeared to and the second ones looked like they'd passed through a thousand wars. They had strange things attached to them, sticky things, and they seemed like they'd been chewed up and torn.

"I'll go back and have them mended," I thought.

The salesman looked at them.

Taking care not to touch them, he spoke in a dubious and troubled voice, "Just look at them! How could he have torn them in such a way?"

"I don't know," I said, distressed by my own ignorance.

"No, there is no fixing these," he said.

"What a shame," I thought, while Atilio waited for me at home under the covers, since he hadn't been able to come along without pants to wear. I had wanted the salesman to raise them toward the light, with a stick, perhaps – but sticks aren't found in shops, so he lifted the cuff with his fingernail to see what unfathomable mystery might be hiding inside those pants.

MY BED AWAY FROM HOME

I AM ADMITTED to the ICU of a small hospital. The walls are lined with beds, which are connected to machines that buzz all day. Two of the machines converse, one says "dum, dum" and the other "piff." The central corridor in front of my bed is like a crowded street where all sorts of people pass by: Colombian residents (guys and girls), physical therapists, radiologists, medical supply stockers, psychologists, cleaning staff, and others I can't remember. In the kitchen, the nurses chop something vigorously and I pretend they're chopping beets and onions (wishful thinking on my part – it sounds like crunching glass.) Often the nurses fail to put up a screen when a patient is using their bedpan or having their diaper changed; once they changed my diaper while a Colombian resident was at the computer and a crowd was passing by me on the street. That corridor reminded me of a Bosch painting, the one with a madman pulling a wagon, a pig on a leash, and a group dancing in the background.

I thought to myself: this place is like a game of Anton Pirulero, or the definition of "having one's ass to the wind."

The ward is mixed, in that it has both male and female patients and that I might be bathed by a male nurse, José, for example, who used to bathe me tenderly at night. He was much better than Nurse María, who always seemed to be in a huff with me. Once I kicked a pillow off the bed while I was doing some exercises to strengthen my feet.

"You threw the pillow," she said severely.

"What'd I do now?" I said, like the kids do. "It fell."

She didn't like when I stretched my legs in bed, as if it were a bad and unsightly act. She seemed to be prone to Platonic thought: that which is ugly must also be bad.

I thought I should be allowed to do whatever I wanted in my own bed, but I guess not. My bed was my homeland, my identity; I called the space between me and the little table the border.

One day Nurse María lightened up and asked if I used to go dancing when I was young. Yes, I told her, but that was so long ago…

"What kind of music do you like? Do you like Vicentico?"

"Yes, of course," I said, "and Calamaro too."

She knew Calamaro and liked him.

I, who knew nothing about Argentine rock, felt proud to have something in common with María and to leave her with a better impression of me.

You could hear a man named Juan yelling while they sprayed his back with a little machine. He was making quite the scene – it didn't seem worthwhile to shout so much over something so trivial, but then again maybe it really did hurt.

"Nooo!" he shouted, "It's not right what you're doing. You people are evil, I'm going to report you all, you'll see, you'll see what happens to you!"

"Take it easy, Juan," the nurse said.

When they were done spraying his back, Juan's tone of voice changed completely – he spoke to them in a friendly voice.

A few steps from my bed (I'm not sure how I caught a glimpse of them, I still wasn't able to walk on my own) a few patients are lying motionless. Nobody utters a sound, except one woman who complains under her breath before letting out a cackle.

When I first arrived, I would hear the nurses say, "Up we go, Maxu, sweetie. What about you Evangelina, are you comfortable?"

"They've admitted some kids," I'd thought to myself, but no, it was the nurses who treated them like kids, and not patients who were sound asleep.

Coca, a student I've known for many years, came to visit me and I told her I was embarrassed for people to see me like that, with my ass to the wind.

"We all have asses, Hebe," she replied soberly.

It was a Socratic truth, the moment when Socrates grasps for universal consensus before continuing his argument.

Indeed, Socrates, we all have asses.

Nurse Andrea tells a mute patient that his face is mahogany, the color of wood.

"Now let's get rid of that beard, my little castaway."

No reply, but she keeps going: "I've been a mother for nine whole years."

Nothing but crickets.

Marcelina, the psychologist, visits me every day for a half-hour long chat. She has soft features and is beautiful, a beauty that does not register immediately but manifests in her selflessness. There's no sign of restraint behind her light blue eyes, no prickly look. Her husband must love her in silence. The residents are mostly Colombian, and then there's Doctor José, who is constantly passing by on the corridor in front of my bed. He is a man of low stature, but he covers great distances. He crosses the entire wing with the gait of a little old man (he's probably in his early thirties). Nothing fazes him. I've watched him sift through files for long stretches of time while exercising in my red sweatpants. It's as if he were in the throes of some scientific mission, delivering stacks of medical records from one wing to the next. His hairstyle is strange, a triangular chufa plant that sprouts from his Mayan forehead. I am certain of his Mayan heritage. He doesn't make friends with anyone. He's married to another resident, a Colombian woman who is equally small and serious. I didn't picture him being married – married people are more flexible, they go with the flow, they change. Doctor José desires to be nothing more than a tool for science, he clutches his precious stack of folders against his chest, level to his heart. He goes up to other Colombian doctors who hardly look at the files before tossing them on the sofa or elsewhere, as if to say, "Shit looks fine to me." They don't value José's devotion, they scold him and then laugh about it with Ervin, a nurse who spends his afternoons joking around.

Once I was with Ervin and Marcela, another nurse who is always looking for Ervin because he's off joking in some other room. The group was Ervin, Marcela in her tiny gnome boots, JuHo, the physical therapist, and me. A debate arose around the subject of gender-neutral language and the use of "Elles" and "Nosotres."

"What's your take on 'Elles'?" Julio asks me.

As usual, I don't have a reply, or rather it doesn't ring a bell, but to avoid seeming ignorant or behind the times, I say, "It's the new thing."

"With so many important things to think about, why worry about that nonsense," says Ervin.

But Marcela, in her gnome boots, says, "Yet here we are, the four of us, two and two, and we can't say "nosotras" because "nosotros" is worth more – it's men who are valued more."

Aldo the physical therapist likes professions that are not his own and is always there when doctors make their rounds, he's a jack of all trades.

Some of the nurses are severe, dogmatic types who frequently adjust diapers and forbid me from walking without a physical therapist present. I am allowed only brief walks with an oxygen tube, nothing more. Stuck inside the ward, I visit the other patients.

One nurse speaks to a man who is beyond good and evil, "Juan, cough like a gentleman!"

"You have deceptive veins," they tell another patient, "All for show and impossible to prick."

Nearby, a woman tilts her head, a gesture that seems robotic. They are giving her an electric shock.

She says "Ow, it hurts!" and the nurse replies, "Bend your neck, that's it, all done, you've had dirt behind your ears since the nuns bathed you."

"I'm about to fall, nurse."

"Fall into hygiene. Now, open your mouth, don't be bullheaded."

The patient's head is tilted to the right, and they want her to straighten it, but she doesn't seem to care if she sees the world horizontally or straight on. There is no logic to the nurses' observations, they say things like "Let me clean your tongue, it's all green" or "Open your mouth, don't be such a liar," followed up by "You're an angel."

I am reading *Biographies of Illustrious Men* while I watch and listen to all of this. Charlemagne, Goethe, etc. It's written by Thomas de Quincey. In theory, the life of Goethe is fascinating, but I've always found it boring to read. In his biography, Thomas de Quincey writes, "There can be no gloomier form of infidelity than that which questions the moral attributes of the Great Being, in whose hands are the final destinies of us all."

MAKE YOURSELVES USEFUL

In the presence of slackers or idleness, some people say, "Make yourselves useful." I used to dismiss this statement, but after being confined to my bed all day, it began to make sense. In a hospital bed, you turn into an unrecognizable tyrant who wants someone to pick up the reading glasses you dropped on the floor, or take away the leftovers from breakfast, or hand you the cream (simply because you're bored), or lead you somewhere by the hand, or cover your feet because the blanket slid off and you can't reach that far, or find someone to talk national and global politics with you, or anything for that matter.

I am bound to be a tyrant, but it befits me to be a shrewd one. When a nurse is nearby, I must ask her for two or three things at once, but not in the same breath, I must be calm and measured – if I say I want this, this, and that, it will seem like I'm demanding too much. At some point I turned into a bit of a Nazi. The nurses would attend first to those people who were silent as plants and couldn't respond or barely did, meanwhile I would be lucid and waiting, believing I had more rights than they did. The nurses wouldn't let me stand on my own, they were afraid I might fall. My bed was blocked in by two doors and I couldn't get out without someone's help. Doctor Ángel, a Colombian man with big, mischievous eyes, came by one afternoon. He had a voice that spilled forth, radiating from deep within him, below his throat. It was a very pleasant voice, I came to think of it as the voice of the rainforest. We talked about national and global politics.

You spend most of your time there waiting. For the food to be brought in, for a visitor to arrive, or checking one's phone for the tenth time, for the time to pass. Everything happens inside a shrunken, repetitive world, at an arm's reach. I am reminded of the fates of the Cumaean Sibyl and Tithonus, who begged the gods to grant them immortality, but forgot to ask for eternal youth. So each of them walks in little circles around themselves, always doing the same nonsense.

I was nervously awaiting the pulmonologist. We hadn't yet met, but people spoke of her as if she might appear at any time of day or night. To prepare for her visit, I didn't eat all day, and at seven in the evening, she descended like a cyclone. She had the momentum of a train engine and the movements of a magician; within two seconds she had stuffed her thick viny waves into an old cap. She began explaining this and that and writing on a nearby whiteboard, in another two seconds, three disciples appeared, circling her, and she spoke to all three of them at full speed. It resembled a theater production. She had me swallow two drugs whose taste was inconceivable, and she pushed a tube through my nose and down to my lungs. My throat was asleep, so I didn't feel anything. She told me that I was very brave, although I would have much rather heard her say that everything was in order down there. I didn't ask her anything about my lungs – it was good enough, after all, to be brave.

CHANGE OF SCENERY

I spent all of my time in the ICU thinking of the bathroom and its whereabouts, as though it were London or Paris. After being transferred to Intermediate Care, they situated me near an EXIT sign which, to my great joy, was directly beside a bathroom. I felt as though I had been promoted, and what's more, I also began taking walks along an external corridor with the help of several meters of rope. There I spoke to people in passing; upon reaching the kitchen, I would ask the cook for the menu of the day.

Intermediate Care was for the most part better than the ICU and in other ways it was worse. It was better because, although people shrieked in pain, they at least produced some sort of noise. I found out that Juan had been transferred to the same ward when I heard him shouting "I'm going to report you!" Nearby, a patient was shrieking like a frightened animal. They were setting her up with a feeding tube:

"How long have you gone without eating?" the nurse asked.

"Two months," she said, in an unhinged voice.

"If you pull out this tube," the nurse said, "I've got fifty others waiting for you. You think you're the pain in the ass around here, well, I'm an even bigger one. Better calm down before things take a turn for the worse."

This ward is worse than my previous one, or I prefer it less. It has long white curtains surrounding most beds and seems like a hospital from the 19th century, where nurses in floor-length skirts and frilly bonnets might appear at any moment. My previous ward was a circus (everyone and their mother would rush by through the corridor) but at least it was a circus from the 21st century. In this ward, we are often visited by the head nurse, a dark-haired playboy who owns two beautiful sweaters: one red, the other blue.

When he is present and I think she doesn't see him, crazy Justa doesn't make ugly noises, as if she's on her best behavior. When the head nurse leaves, she makes noises that come straight from the gutter.

I am reading Alfredo Bryce Echenique's latest stories, from 2014. I've enjoyed several of Bryce's earlier books because of his command of language – his writing feels free and he sometimes comes up with delightful expressions. But I didn't enjoy his last book because it's as if he's relied on sly tricks to lengthen his stories, and it all sounds a bit forced. I prefer to look around instead.

MY BEDSIDE NEIGHBORS

Near the middle of the room (which for some reason or other doesn't have curtains) a bus driver says his son sold his bus for 20,000 pesos and that he's going to report him to the police. Every few minutes, he says he's going to go to the police station. He says all this to Alfredo, who is in a bed nearby. Alfredo is a very slight and cautious man – if he had been born in the rainforests of Peru his name would have been "Quiverin' Mouse." Not once have I ever heard him pass judgment, not even when some physical therapists kept him waiting for hours before accompanying him on a walk. He entertains himself by looking for new words in the dictionary. Why doesn't he call on Aldo, the physical therapist, to check on him? Why doesn't he say anything when Aldo flees? He says he's going to fetch a walker but takes so long it's as if he's gone to the Far East. Might he believe in the efficacy of God's word or in magical-religious thinking? "If I think negatively, Aldo won't come get me – I must send out positive energy," he must say to himself. In a loud voice, harsh as a thug's,

Osvaldo the bus driver tells Quiverin' Mouse about the bus, but it's hard to understand him because he had a stroke.

Shy little Don Alfredo says, "I imagine you're emotionally attached to the bus, too."

Osvaldo looks at him blankly.

Early in the morning, around four, they give us all EKGs and Osvaldo, who is ranting about his bus and his swindler son, suddenly yells, "Fucking nurses! Are you out of your minds? An EKG at 4 in the morning? Chiche, Coco, take me to the police station, I'm going to report them!"

Nurse: "Chiche's not coming. Can't you see she's not coming?"

The day before, I had asked the nurse to put up a screen because Osvaldo was looking at me while I was in a diaper.

The nurse replied, "How can you worry about a man who doesn't know his own name, not to mention how he got here?"

Another time, a Colombian resident said to Osvaldo in passing, "Speak clearly, can't you see it's hard to understand you?"

A nurse who overheard him said, "The doctor would do well to take his own advice."

Later, a 96-year-old woman by the name of Ogarina Pia Romana was assigned a bed directly in front of mine. She was all right in the head.

"I'm obsessed with clothes," she tells me. "How is it that my son didn't bring me any? At home, I have a feather mattress."

She used to be a drawing teacher and said that she had painted a portrait last year of a pensive General San Martín before the battle of Maipú. Every step of his armies originated in his mind. After Señora Ogarina left, they put a 102-year-old woman in her place.

She would say: "I'm deaf in this ear and in the other too." She would also sing Alberto Castillo songs, the one that goes "Siga el baile, siga el baile al compás del tamboril." She'd ruminate in bed, taking stock of her life.

Once, she said to the nurse, "Heal me with words."

NURSE SARA

One morning, Sara called her supervisor on the phone:

"Señor Marini, I don't have an assistant today, he called in sick."

Then she turned to face all of us, "No one walks, is that clear? No one on their feet causing trouble."

Sure, it was ten of us patients she had to oversee, and she had a lot to do for certain ones, feed them by hand, adjust their tubes, clean them.

She looked at us again, adding, "And nobody bathes today."

When she came by to give me my pill I, believing myself to be an obedient woman, the model of good behavior, said, "I bathed earlier this morning."

"What's it to me?" she said.

She put safety rails around my bed so I wouldn't get any absurd ideas, like going for a walk. That was around the time the 102-year-old-woman was my bedside neighbor. Sara, brightening up a little, started talking to the woman.

"Are you from Rome?" Sara asked.

"Who are you?"

"I'm the nurse who's taking care of you. Be still, relax."

"Kiss me goodnight."

COMING HOME

A writer friend, Eduardo, was the one who took me to the hospital one evening, after I told him I was feeling weak.

"Why don't we call the ER?" he said, and I figured we would go and come right back, but that was the day they checked me in.

Eduardo was also the one who checked me out and accompanied me all the way home. I never got a clear sense of Dr. Arenas, who authorized my departure. He oversaw visits between residents and patients; the residents would describe each patient's condition while Dr. Arenas listened distractedly, touching the fabric of the sofa while they spoke, as though he would have preferred to be somewhere else, in some other line of work. I thought I might spend the rest of my life in that hospital bed, and I was a little anxious about coming home. Who knew what that next stage of life would bring? Once we got to the ambulance, I sat in front of Eduardo, and the fact that I was on a chair instead of a stretcher seemed like a step in the right direction. I wasn't very pleased about going home – I've always feared the new. It took us a while to arrive because the ambulance got stuck in traffic, but if we'd been held up even longer, it would have been fine by me.

All of a sudden, I noticed a yellowish stone wall.

"I know that wall," I said.

It was the apartment building across the street.

My dear students were waiting for me inside, and they had made a few changes. I've always liked having my belongings rearranged, to notice the trace of another's hand, like the time a housekeeper put a little hat on my teapot and hung a flower from its spout. My students had moved a sofa bed into my apartment for whoever would be looking after me, an oxygen tank was waiting for me, too, and someone had organized the towels and sheets in my closet. I tend to toss my towels in there – sometimes I'll throw them from two meters away, how they land is how they remain. But I now had two perfectly distinct stacks of sheets and towels. And I poured everyone a bit of wine I had lying around.

archipelago books
is a not-for-profit literary press devoted to
promoting cross-cultural exchange through innovative
classic and contemporary international literature
www.archipelagobooks.org